DEIDRE BJORSON

The Haunting of Locker 31

For Kris:
Because you always believed in me.
(I told you I wrote stuff.)

Contents

Acknowledgement

Thank you to all the people who helped me along the way in creating this book.

Amy: for reading the very rough first draft.

Caty, Mom, Laura and Robin: For reading the second draft.

My Editor and Cover Designer Nick and Nat: For making my book pretty inside and out.

My husband, Kris, for pushing me, supporting me and making me laugh at myself during all of this. This would never have been more than a dream without you.

Prologue: Prom Night 2000

The music was pounding inside but Lily was outside, throwing up in the dumpster. She hadn't been able to keep anything down for days. It could just be paranoia, but she was pretty certain her mom was growing suspicious. She either knew she was pregnant or thought her daughter had an eating disorder.

After tonight, she could confess. It would be okay. Wiping her mouth with the back of her hand, she righted herself and straightened her dress, which was too tight over her chest. Not how she had pictured her prom night going.

"There you are!" Brian stepped outside. He looked gorgeous in this light. There was very little light that he didn't look amazing in. Too bad she didn't love him anymore.

"Sorry, I just needed some fresh air." She moved closer to him to avoid the smell coming from the dumpster.

Brian grabbed her waist and moved her against the wall. "I figured you wanted me to follow you out here."

"Oh, Brian, not out here by the dumpsters. That's gross!"

He ignored her protests, kissing her neck. She needed to sleep with Brian tonight for the plan to work. She let him grab her butt while she counted how many days she would need to wait to tell him. She wished she had paid more attention in health class. His mouth came close to hers and she pushed him away playfully. "Not right now! Later! I want it to be special."

He grumbled, unable to make words of protest, but then nodded. They returned inside and she excused herself to the restroom. She moved to the sink and rinsed out her mouth, spraying some mint spray to hide the vomit smell.

"Hey! You okay?" Shannon came into the room. Her hair was twice its normal size, and her skin did not go with the puffy-sleeved dark green dress. Her hair only added to the porkiness of her face. Everyone at school wondered why they were friends. They made such an odd pair. But Shannon had a good heart, and they had been friends since day one of kindergarten.

"Yeah. Kind of queasy."

"Do you think this plan will work?"

"It has to. Besides, we both know that Brian is good-looking but not the brightest."

"True." Shannon checked herself in the mirror. Lily lent her friend her lipstick and pulled up the strap that had slipped down her shoulder.

"Better get out there. Don't want to miss the greatest night of our lives!"

Lily managed not to throw up while they danced. She and Brian were slowly swaying back and forth after the Queen and King had been crowned. Lost in thought, it took a second for her to realize that Brian was talking to her.

"Are you okay?"

"Yeah! Just thinking."

"About what?"

Lily smiled and ground her body into Brian's. "All the things I want to do to you."

"Baby, you can't do that and then ask me to wait." He pulled her tight against him.

"Let's get out of here, then."

"Gladly." He took her hand and dragged her out of the party. Lily flashed a smile at Shannon, who was standing against the wall before ducking out of the gym. She laughed as they raced to his Mustang. Lily knew very little about cars, but she knew looks and the looks other boys gave Brian when he pulled up in this car made her glad she was with him. They didn't leave the parking lot. She pulled up her dress and straddled him in the front seat.

"Oh, man!" He panted as she slipped back over into her side. Relief washed over her and the weight of one problem left her. "Baby, why did we wait to do that!"

"It needed to be special!" She pulled down the mirror and fixed her hair, her lipstick. When she finished, she looked back at him. He was not smiling at her.

"Did it hurt?"

"What?"

"Did it hurt?"

"Brian, what on earth are you on about?"

"It's supposed to hurt the first time. For a girl."

"Who said that?"

"Did it hurt?" He already knew the answer. He threw open his car door. "Together for two years! We break up for a couple months and you sleep with someone else! Then you get back with me and act like it had to be special! Screw you!" He slammed the door behind him.

"Brian!" Lily grabbed her shoes and jumped out after him. Not as dumb as she thought. He was out of sight by the time she got her shoes on.

"Damn it!" she cursed. Crossing her arms over her chest, she walked back to the school. Halfway there, she stopped to throw up, leaning between two cars. She cursed again, stomping her foot in frustration, then cursed again at the pain from the high heel racing up her leg and spine.

The pain from the blow to the back of her head was worse. It knocked her to the ground and lights danced around her eyes, just like in Looney Tunes. Instinctively, she crawled and went right through her own vomit. The next blow knocked her into the car.

"Please!" she pleaded. Blood blinded her. "Please, stop!"

The next blow silenced her.

One

Chicago Blues–2020

The table in the room was wobbly. One leg was missing its bottom piece, causing the table to rock anytime someone put weight on it.There was a noticeable scratch down the middle leading to the half hook anchored in the center of the table. The wobbly table with the scratch bothered Misti more than the two-way mirror hiding the eyes that were watching her write. The table wobbled with every stroke of the pen, making her handwriting sloppy. She knew they were in there, discussing her fate. She stopped writing and looked at the mirror, hiding any emotion on her face.

"I'm done." She dropped the pen and pushed the yellow legal pad away, hiding the scratch the best she could. She crossed her arms and cradled her elbows. The door to the room opened and Detective Sanders and Ms. Webb entered. Detective Sanders took the notepad and scanned what she had written. Misti watched him out of the corner of her eye, focusing on the stupid scratch again. She hoped he didn't need her to rewrite it. If it was too sloppy, it wasn't her fault. They needed a better table.

"Misti, do you have any family? Anyone in the city?" Ms. Webb asked, pulling out a stack of forms and dropping them on the table. She pulled out the chair on the other side of the table.

"No." The table rocked as Ms. Webb waited, clicking a pen and writing in fine print on the first form.

MISTI BOYLE

AGE 17

"Do you know of any family? Anywhere? We really prefer to place children with family."

"I have an aunt, down south. In Colorado. I haven't seen her in a while." Maybe ten years. Maybe less. Misti remembered the town. Remembered her aunt. She was nothing like her sister.

"Do you know her name?"

"Mary McCarthy."

Ms. Webb wrote down the name carefully. She seemed to be oblivious to the table. Her handwriting was perfect. Misti turned her eyes away from the government forms and focused on the detective. He was on the third page of her statement. Had she really written that much?

"What's going to happen to my mom?"

Detective Sanders looked up at her, his dark eyes sharp even with his graying hair and deep wrinkles. "She's going to prison."

"She needs to go to a mental hospital." Both adults raised their eyebrows at her. "I'm not making excuses for what she did. But a prison isn't going to help her." Misti lost her voice and her eyes fell back on the table.

"That is for the court to decide." Detective Sanders tucked the notepad under his arm and patted Misti on the shoulder. "The statement is great. I know it must have been hard."

Misti didn't look up at him, gripping her elbows harder. The clock above the door was hanging askew. Almost as annoying as the wobbly

2

table. It was just after 4am.

Ms. Webb rose and followed him, saying nothing to Misti. Misti stared at the table, ignoring the sandwich someone had offered her hours earlier and the soda sitting in a pool of condensation. Outside, she kept her face neutral. Inside, she was plotting her escape. She didn't need the state to take care of her. They hadn't been concerned for the last seventeen years. Now didn't seem like the time to be concerned. The clock kept ticking. First ten minutes went by. Then twenty. Finally an hour. Ms. Webb returned and sat down without a word. Misti couldn't decide if she liked the woman. She lacked the empathy that most of the social workers Misti had dealt with had. She didn't fawn over her, hug her, continually touch her. She just asked her an occasional question. Misti wanted to sketch her. Make her look like a witch; a misunderstood one. She kept children locked up in her house, but gave them everything they needed. Not to eat them or anything like that. Just to try to keep them safe.

"I can just stay here." Misti felt the words bubble out of her. "I can just keep working and finish school. I turn eighteen in June."

"Until you are eighteen, you need to be with an adult." Ms. Webb stopped writing, pursing her lips at Misti. Misti knew she looked a mess. The two-way window was a great mirror. Her hair was disheveled and her dark eyeliner smeared.

"I got a hold of your aunt and uncle. They have agreed to take you."

Misti felt like sixty pounds of weights had been taken off her shoulders and now put in her stomach. She did not want to be a burden.

"You called them at 4 in the morning to talk to them?"

Ms. Webb glanced at her watch. She seemed startled by the time. "I guess I did." She sniffed, unconcerned.

Ms. Webb and Detective Sanders escorted Misti back to the apartment.

The daylight had drawn a bigger crowd. There were two officers standing guard at the stairs, nodding a hello to the adults and offering sad smiles to Misti as they climbed the stairs past them. The music from the first floor apartment had been turned off for the first time since Misti had lived there. The stairs were bustling with people. On the second floor, the light had been fixed. Misti had been asking the super to fix that light for three months.

"It might be best to keep your eyes focused on me." Detective Sanders stopped outside the police tape and accepted the blue shoe covers. He handed a pair to Misti. She put them on while the lab tech called for everyone to take five. Several people streamed past the tape, removing the blue covers before plodding down the stairs, some pulling out cigarettes as they went, talking about the Cubs and the hell of a mess they were stepping away from.

"Ready?"

Misti gave one nod. Detective Sanders stepped in first and Misti followed, doing her best to keep her eyes on his back. He knew where he was going and took her to her little room in the back. Her things had clearly been rifled through. Misti dropped to the floor, dragging out well-used suitcases. Sanders shut the door, blocking out the mess in the living room. She grabbed her clothes from the drawer, and from the pile in the corner. Would she have time to wash them before she left? She usually did laundry on Saturday mornings, before work.

"Ms. Webb said you should be on a bus this afternoon heading for Colorado. Never been there. Heard the mountains are something else."

Misti didn't know if that was a question or a statement. She continued to gather her things, hurrying so she didn't waste any more of the detective's time.

"This isn't your fault, you know."

Misti glanced up from her task. Detective Sanders was focusing

4

hard on her.

"She needed help a long time ago. I could've gotten it for her." Misti dropped the makeup bag into her pack. Would they at least let her shower before she got on a bus?

"You're a kid. Should never have been your job to be working as much as you are, taking care of your mom. Should have been the other way around. You should have been out, doing teenage girl stuff. Driving boys crazy, going to dances, seeing movies."

Misti stared at him, unsure of how to respond. Not her job? Of course it had been her job. Her mother needed her to be there. Without her doing all of this, where would they have been? Misti glanced around the room. "That's it, I guess."

Detective Sanders led her out and Misti glanced down once. The blood had ruined the carpet. The lazy building manager would have to replace it.

When they arrived back at the station, Misti asked if she could take a shower somewhere. They escorted her to the women's locker room. A female officer waited outside while she showered quickly. She scrubbed her skin raw and cleaned up her face. She pulled out her makeup and was starting to apply eyeliner when Ms. Webb barged in.

"The bus leaves in an hour." Ms Webb glanced at herself in the mirror, smoothing her bobbed hair. She turned her eye to Misti's thick eyeliner. "Before you go, Misti, I want you to think of this as a new, fresh start." Misti kept applying her makeup. "You could reinvent yourself. Be someone you have always wanted to be but couldn't."

Misti finished her makeup. There was no way to hide the dark circles under her eyes. Sleep would be the only thing that fixed that.

"Did you hear what I said?"

Misti nodded that she had. But really, did she need to take advice from Ms. Webb, the robot woman?

They stepped out into the hall together. Detective Sanders was talking on his phone. He ended the conversation and approached them.

"Do you want to see your mom? Say goodbye?" he asked her.

Misti shifted the messenger bag on her shoulder and looked from adult to adult. "No. I have a bus to catch."

Two

The Arrival

⚛

The bus was running late. The bus always ran late and the McGraths knew this. They had only been waiting a few minutes when it came rumbling down the road, hissing as it came to a stop in the quiet, eerily lit terminal. It was just after 9 in the morning. Mr. McGrath rose as the bus doors opened. He waited as a figure moved down the aisle and stepped onto the platform.

Misti wore plain jeans, an oversized zippered hoodie that had tattered sleeves and the remnants of a logo, and black lace boots rolled down a little; she could have been in a 1990s grunge band. Her denim messenger bag was slung over her shoulder and her arms were crossed over her chest. Mrs. McGrath took in a short breath. The girl looked so much like her mother.

"Aunt Mary?" Her voice was flat and toneless.

"Yes, dear! Oh, Misti!" Mrs. McGrath flung her arms around the girl, hugging her. She loomed over her niece by a full half a foot, and had broad shoulders and wide hips that swayed when she walked. The older woman's temples were graying and laugh lines created shallow canyons around her mouth and forehead. "Here we are."

"I'm sorry the bus ran late," Misti pulled away from the hug without returning it. "I didn't want to keep you waiting."

"Oh my dear, that's okay!" Mrs. McGrath patted her arm, looking at her husband for his response.

"No problem at all," he said. He moved to the driver, who had pulled out two bags and dropped them at his feet. The driver tipped his hat at the girl before jumping back into the empty bus and driving away.

"This everything?"

"Yes. I didn't want to bring too much," Misti heard herself lie.

"Oh, you couldn't have brought too much!" Mrs. McGrath touched her again as if to confirm her existence. Anxiety flooded Misti's face. She took a step back, gripping her elbows in opposite hands. Mrs. McGrath pulled her hand back, blushing.

"Let's get you home." Mr. McGrath personified the former football star: well built, with strong-looking arms beginning to sag and a middle to match. He lifted the bags with a huff before leading the way out of the terminal. The girl stood in place, her eyes going towards the bus moving out of sight.

"Come along, dear." Mrs. McGrath put her arm around the girl. She did not pull away this time. She allowed her aunt to lead her out of the building and to the waiting SUV. They loaded her into the back seat, much like a person who might be in witness protection.

"Are you hungry? We can stop and get something if you'd like?" Mrs. McGrath asked, examining her as she buckled her seat belt.

"I'm okay."

Mr. McGrath finished loading the bags and got into the car. They rolled out of the parking lot, heading through main street.

It was the most American main street Misti had ever seen—brick shops and American flags flying at every doorway. Misti noted an antique store, a bookstore, a music store, a coffee shop, another antique store, an ice cream shop, and a bistro. It looked as if it belonged in a Disney movie. She watched people walking down the street, stopping and talking to others. Misti noticed an old man reading a paper at the coffee shop, and a little girl in a red dress skipping down the road clinging to a teddy bear ahead of her parents who held hands. She studied a group of teenagers heading into the music store.

Welcome to Blackwood, Colorado! Home of the Fighting Tigers!

No wonder her mother had left this town and never looked back.

"Kids from school like to hang out down here on weekends. Penny, your cousin, can't wait to take you on a tour and introduce you!" Mrs. McGrath shifted in the front seat. She seemed nervous. "Penny went to school today. She wanted to come with us today, but she had a particularly important test in her AP government class. But she'll come right after school. We took the day off." Guilt filled Misti's chest. "I work at the bank as a teller and your Uncle Bill here works as an electrician. He's going back to work this afternoon, but I'll be home all day with you so you don't have to be alone. I thought we could get your room all set up and then take you to the school to get registered." She stopped for air, eyeing a group of women wearing walking clothes—tight, calf-length black pants and tighter bright-colored tank tops—all looking exceedingly serious as they swung their arms and wiggled their hips to keep pace with the long-legged and lean leader. Mrs. McGrath smoothed her clothes absentmindedly, touching her hair.

"That's nice of you," Misti said, bringing her aunt back into the car. "I don't want to be a bother."

"You are most certainly not a bother!" she said, too firmly for Misti to believe. Mr. McGrath had said nothing since starting the drive. Misti wondered if he ever got a word in edgewise. Mrs. McGrath must have caught her tone because she changed the subject. "We couldn't be happier to have you. Our home is your home."

9

The tone shifted. Misti could still sense a hint of tension. Perhaps if Uncle Bill would say something— agree with her—Misti would believe it. But he kept his eyes on the road, a blank face, hands at 2 and 10. Silence fell upon the car and Misti focused on the houses they glided past. Each one occupied two stories with perfect green yards and trimmed hedges. Some houses were white, some blue, some green. Each had been decorated for the fall, with cute pumpkins stacked together with hay and a few miniature scarecrows. Each home had "Welcome" signs instead of broken-down cars.

The house they pulled into fit right in with the rest of the neighborhood: two stories and an immaculate front lawn. The grass had begun to fade around the edges. Orange and white and yellow pumpkins littered the front porch. The door held a wreath of pinecones and leaves and burlap. A large sign leaning against the side of the house said "Welcome!" in a pretty font. It looked like it belonged in a magazine.

"I decorated it myself," Mrs. McGrath said. The pride in her voice forced Misti to give a small nod of approval. It looked just like all the others they had passed.

Mr. McGrath carried the suitcases in as Mrs. McGrath led the way through the wooden door. Inside, the house smelled clean, with a hint of cinnamon. The floors sparkled, and family pictures hung along the wall. There were four empty hooks on the wall. Mrs. McGrath removed her coat and hung it up. She also slipped off her shoes and put them away. She looked at Misti, who slipped out of her shoes, took off her black jacket and hung it up. Mr. McGrath came in behind them, huffing again. He dropped the cases and let out a loud sigh.

"I can take them now." Misti moved to the little bag, but Mr. McGrath waved her off.

"It's okay; she'll want to give you a tour."

Mrs. McGrath smiled and then escorted Misti through the hall past the stairs. They entered a large room that served as both the family room and the kitchen. The kitchen sparkled, and the counters contained no clutter. A cream-colored sectional pointed at a large TV, while a fireplace completed the cozy family living space. Misti hated how comfortable this entire place felt. "This is nice," she said.

Mrs. McGrath beamed with pride. "We spend most of our time in this room. We have all our meals as a family. Most nights, we eat at the island, but for important meals we eat in the dining room."

The dining room looked over the backyard. Its large table with eight chairs looked brand new. Misti wondered what constituted an important meal.

Misti repeated her words from earlier. Although she knew this was important to her hostess, Misti wanted to go lie down. She had been on a bus for two days, and she had gotten little sleep. She knew she wouldn't be able to control her emotions on little sleep, and she needed to control her emotions. She couldn't risk making a bad impression. This would be home for the next eight months until she turned 18.

They continued with the tour, looking over the plain backyard with a little lawn and a shed. It looked unused. They traveled back to the front and Misti noticed a side room set up as an office.

"You and Penny can use that to do your homework. Although the schools give their students computers now, so it just sits empty. Except during fantasy football—then you can't get Bill out of there." Mrs. McGrath had relaxed, helping Misti to relax too. They moved upstairs, and she toured the bathroom she would share with Penny. A hair straightener and curler had been left on the counter, along with eyeliner. Mrs. McGrath pursed her lips in annoyance.

"Teenagers! Always sleeping as long as they can; they don't give themselves time to get ready." Mrs. McGrath lingered and Misti watched the debate of her wanting to put the items away or just continue with the tour. Mrs. Mcgrath moved down the hall, opening a door. Penny's room. Not as organized as the rest of the house, but it held a made-up bed and clean floor. She then moved across the hallway and opened another door. "This is your room."

The room contained only a bed and a dresser. Nothing hung from the wall. A blank canvas.

"We can paint it any color you want. Hang curtains you like, get a headboard. Whatever you want or need."

Misti's bags sat next to the bed. A wave of fear crashed over her. "Okay," she said, almost choking on the word.

"Mary," Mr. McGrath emerged from the other end of the hall. The master bedroom, Misti assumed. He had dressed in different clothes. He was on his way to work. "Why don't you let her have a few minutes to herself? Let her take a nap? I haven't been on a bus in a long time, but I'm sure they're about as restful now as they were then."

"Oh, of course!" Mrs. McGrath looked startled and a little embarrassed that she hadn't thought about that. "You take as long as you need. I'll be downstairs."

Misti managed a smile before stepping into the room and closing the door. She listened on the other side as they moved down the stairs in their socks. She heard murmuring, but could not understand it. Misti took off her sweater and let it plop to the floor. Her mother had not insisted on a clean floor. Instead, she was the one who had picked things up. She touched the bedding and stroked the soft fabric for a moment, forgetting where she was for a second. She lifted the covers and slid into the bed and felt as if she were on a cloud. The sleep that had eluded her for the past several weeks found her now.

Three

New Chance

Misti sat up with a jolt. The afternoon sunlight hit the window, casting a tranquil autumn glow. It took a moment for her to recall where she was and steady her mind. She drew a couple deep breaths and let go of the blankets in her grasp. Her hair was sticky and her clothes clung to her. She studied the clock on the bedside stand. 3:52. Oops. She had slept away most of the day.

And she was ravenous. Misti swung her feet to the floor, noting the lush carpet. She laid the blankets back over, attempting to recreate the hotel-like folds. It didn't look half bad. Didn't matter. She would be crawling back into bed in a few hours. It would just get messy again. The reason her mother said they never made the beds. She gave the same excuse for not doing dishes. Or laundry.

Misti looked into the mirror on her dresser and grimaced. Her dark makeup and hair were a wreck again. At least the dark circles under her eyes had faded. Turning to the denim bag she had brought with her, she dug out her hairbrush and a smaller patchwork bag. She opened the door and listened. She could pick up the murmur of the

TV downstairs. Missing one sock, she cut across to the bathroom and closed the door. She needed to take a shower, but she chose to wait until before bed.

Misti brushed her thick wavy hair before getting out a makeup wipe. She cleaned off her makeup and hesitated. She had never considered herself an ugly girl. She thought she had a nice nose. But she never saw herself as pretty. At her other schools, she just blended in. She avoided having an issue with others. She enjoyed playing the part of an anonymous background character.

Her mother always encouraged the dark makeup and edgy demeanor. A few months before, her mother tried cutting off all her hair to give her a pixie cut. Misti refused to let her. It was an ugly fight. Misti winced, her dark eyes finding the few chunks of hair that were a little shorter than the rest.

Instead of reapplying the dark makeup, she opted for only a little eyeliner and some mascara. She didn't recognize herself. And she actually liked that. Maybe Ms. Webb had been onto something back in the locker room. Perhaps here she could rediscover herself, reinvent herself. Instead of being the new girl or the quiet girl or the girl with the crazy mom…. Misti sighed. Here she would be the poor girl living with her aunt and uncle. Girl with a crazy mom might be better.

Tucking the brush and makeup bag under her arm, she stepped back to the door and opened it to meet a girl her age standing on the other side, hand lifted to knock.

She was taller than Misti, with red-brown hair curled just perfectly at the ends. She was slim, with broad shoulders and well-built thighs. She had her mother's eyes and her father's nose. This must be her cousin, Penny. Misti had a flash of memory. She and Penny playing dress up in the bathroom, pretending to be princesses. They had had so much fun. 17 year old Penny still looked the wide eyed girl in the purple princes dress. Just grown up. Misti wondered how much she had changed?

"Hi! Sorry to bother you, but Mom wanted me to check on you and see if you were up yet and hungry at all." She spoke quickly. Nervous. "I'm Penny, by the way, your new roommate!" She giggled at her own joke, flipping her hair.

Misti attempted to smile. She had once read about ways to make people like you. Smiling was important. It hurt her face to try.

"I could eat," Misti said. "I just need to put these away."

"Oh, here!" Penny stepped past her into the bathroom and opened a drawer. It was empty. "I made room for you. I needed to clear out a bunch of ancient junk anyway. I still owned butterfly hair clips!" She rolled her eyes at herself, adjusting her hair in the mirror.

A drawer and a bedroom. This might not be the worst place in the world.

"Thanks," Misti said, depositing her brush and her makeup back into the drawer.

"Mom made some cookies," Penny said, heading for the stairs. Misti followed, realizing halfway down that she still wore only one sock. She stopped and yanked it off and set it down on her boots. Next to her coat hung a dark jacket and a backpack. Penny's things. Uncle Bill's coat was gone.

"Ah! You're awake! Are you hungry? I made some cookies." Aunt Mary pointed to an oval plate of cookies, arranged in a perfect pattern with equal sized cookies all around. Penny hopped up on one of the bar stools and picked up two cookies. Misti sat and lifted one cookie. "Milk?" Both girls nodded. The cookie was delicious.

"Are you feeling refreshed? How did you like the bed?"

"It's the most comfortable I've ever slept on!" Misti said after swallowing her cookie with a gulp of milk. The milk wasn't close to being expired. Aunt Mary beamed. "I'm sorry I slept all afternoon; I know you wanted to get some things done."

15

"Don't be silly. We can get you registered tomorrow. I don't have to work until 10 on Wednesdays." Aunt Mary topped off both their milks and returned the glass bottle to the fridge. Misti looked at Penny, who offered her an encouraging grin.

"Penny also advised me that you're seventeen and don't need someone to help decorate your room if you don't wish it. And that you possibly have your own decorations to hang up."

Misti worried about her suitcases upstairs. They held all the clothes she owned. Most of those had been tired when she bought them at the thrift store; she would need new ones soon. There was her sketchbook, her pencils, and charcoal. A couple pictures. A few movies and a few books. Nothing to hang on the walls. She had never been in one place long enough to hang items on the wall.

"You could help me if you want. I don't have much." Misti looked at her glass and blushed.

Mary seemed to perk up again and smirked at her daughter. "Well, supper is already in the crockpot, so let's go get you unpacked and see what we're working with. You coming, Penny?"

"Sure. I can't help long, I have stupid math homework again."

"Homework is not stupid!" Mary said, already halfway up the stairs.

"Calculus is," Penny whispered to Misti before grinning and dashing up the stairs. Misti grabbed one more cookie and her sock before rushing after them. The light was on and Mary had swung the first suitcase up onto the bed. She did not open it. Instead she opened the closet door and a few drawers in the dresser.

Misti opened the suitcase and let it fall back. Although it was a large suitcase, it contained very little. While she pulled out her sketchbook and her pencils, she saw Penny and Mary exchange glances.

"I didn't bring much," Misti heard herself lying. She didn't know how to tell them that this was all that she had in the world and that moving in two suitcases had been a regular thing for her. Nothing new there.

Having her own room and eating homemade cookies that she didn't have to worry about being laced with something a little stronger than chocolate was different. Her bed was comfortable and the cleanest she had ever slept on. An uncomfortable silence pressed down on the room as they started taking out her clothes. Mary attempted to keep a neutral face but Penny did not. She looked startled, disgusted, and sad. Misti regretted allowing them to help. She took notice of their clothes for the first time and saw that, although they were not designer, her aunt and cousin were the original owners.

"What's the school like?" Misti asked, attempting to divert attention. It worked on Penny.

"It's like most high schools, I suppose. We only have one gym but most schools have two now. We just had a homecoming. The teachers are really good for the most part. Except Mr. Hill. He's worthless."

"Penny," Mary scolded, while she refolded Misti's shirts to inspect them. Misti wanted to snatch her things, throw them all into the suitcase in a messy pile and run for it.

"Well, it's true! He won't move on in teaching until everyone agrees with him that the Moon landing is fake!" Misti must have made the right face because Penny continued eagerly. Aunt Mary put the shirts in the drawer. "Like, seriously. I refused to admit it and we wasted three weeks of sophomore year watching stupid YouTube videos about the conspiracy theories surrounding the Moon landing. Dad finally told me to just say that I believed so we would learn a little biology before Christmas."

Misti only had the pants she had on and one other pair that Aunt Mary set carefully in the drawer. Perhaps she thought they would crumble in her hands.

"Why don't they fire him?" Misti asked, closing her now empty suitcases.

"They won't. He's the basketball coach and our team has almost made it to state for the last three years or something like that." Mary took the bags from Misti and tucked them up on the top shelf in the closet. "After dinner, we can go through my yearbooks and I can show you a little. I'm the yearbook editor. I have them all from the last three years!" Penny looked around and sighed. "I guess I'll go do my homework."

Misti wanted to smile. The girl sounded defeated.

"You'll live, Penny," Mary said. She did not seem to pity her daughter in the least.

"Are you a math genius, Misti?" Penny sounded hopeful.

"No. Math is my worst subject."

"Mine too!" Penny paused. "Maybe you'll be in my class and then we can suffer through together!"

Misti nodded, but she would never be able to handle calculus. And she secretly didn't want classes with her cousin. This first day chit-chat did not mean they would be friends. It would be hard if they got close and Misti left. Because that was the plan. Although this place was nice and comfortable and safe, she was not going to stay here.

Misti went back downstairs with her aunt. Mary turned on the news and puttered around in the kitchen. Misti offered to help twice, but Mary waved her away, telling her to relax.

A long silence occurred between them. Misti felt her aunt watching her, not the news. Misti did not watch the news either; she waited for something, anything, to happen.

"Misti?"

Misti recognized that tone. She was about to be asked serious questions. She suddenly wished she had stayed in her room. She must have tensed because Mary moved and sat next to her. Not touching her, but she could simply reach out a little and there would be contact. "I'm not going to ask anything. The social worker explained most of it over the phone. I just want you to know that if you ever want to talk about what happened, I'm here."

Misti relaxed and pulled her eyes away from the TV. Her aunt had the same eyes as her mother, only calm and sincere. "Thanks, Aunt Mary," Misti said. She was okay. Despite what everyone kept saying. Because what happened was over. And no amount of pondering or talking about it would change that. She had always been waiting for it to happen. It was a release when it did. Not a relief, because it was terrible. But she was glad it did happen. Mary smiled at her, patted her knee a few times and moved back to the kitchen.

Uncle Bill came home just after 5. He greeted his wife with a kiss and nodded a hello to Misti before going upstairs to change. Misti and her aunt watched the news until he came back twenty minutes later, freshly showered. He told them about the mess of the building he was working on that week, replacing the old knob and tube wiring with today's standard. He complained about someone named Andrew.

Just before 6, Penny emerged from her room, looking a little flustered, but she confirmed her homework was complete for the night. She didn't think she had done any good on the problems and would probably be failing the test on Friday.

They sat down just after 6, the TV on mute at the island. They ate roasted chicken, carrots, and mashed potatoes. Misti couldn't help but take a second helping.

Penny filled her in on the school gossip. "Amelia Hopkins supposedly snuck out on Saturday night and didn't come home until Sunday afternoon. She spent the whole time with her boyfriend, Michael Anderson."

Misti perceived that this should be shocking, but teenage girls spending weekends away from home was not something unfamiliar to her.

"Shame on her parents for not going out to find her," Aunt Mary said. "If either of you did that, Bill and I would drive the streets shouting for you until you were so embarrassed you'd never leave the house again."

"Sure, Mother!" Penny rolled her eyes. Misti was not one to sneak out and spend time with her boyfriend. Not that she ever had a boyfriend. She was too busy taking care of her mother to have time for one. And she never really stayed in one place long enough to form the connection she needed.

Misti helped Penny wash and dry dishes and load the dishwasher while Aunt Mary put leftovers into clear containers with colorful lids.

"Are you a buyer of lunch or a taker?" Aunt Mary asked as Misti dried the roasting pan. Misti blinked in confusion. "Do you want to take lunch or buy it there?"

"Take it," Penny said to her. "Lunch is disgusting at our school. Like, the meat is not meat, and the mashed potatoes—and there are always mashed potatoes—taste like cardboard. Don't even get me started on the gravy." She shuttered over dramatically and Misti caught herself smiling again.

"Okay. Pack what you want." Aunt Mary poured herself a large glass of wine and opened a beer bottle before retiring to the sofa to lean against her husband. Penny gagged herself quietly before opening the cupboard for them both. Inside were the most snacks Misti had ever seen. There was jello, pudding, crackers, chips, pretzels, and Cheez-its. Penny grabbed a bag of chips, a jello, and retrieved an apple from the basket on the counter. Misti grabbed a pudding and a Cheez-its bag. She also got the bread and the peanut butter. Penny made herself a ham sandwich while Misti made a classic peanut butter and jelly.

"You should take something for the afternoon, too," Penny said. "Most teachers let you eat in their rooms, as long as you clean up after yourself. The only one who's real…witchy about it is Mrs. Gaillaro. She's a witch about everything."

"Penny!" Aunt Mary said in a sing-song warning voice. Misti took an extra bag of chips and added it to her pile. She watched as Penny dumped a large portion of cereal into a sandwich bag.

"Easy to eat during class."

Misti nodded as if that made perfect sense.

"Is there a paper bag somewhere?"

"Don't be silly." Penny opened one of the island cupboards and produced two lunch bags with pretty designs on them. "Everyone has one of these now."

Misti accepted the bag without hesitation. Heading into a new high school was not something unusual for her, but anything she could do to avoid being a target would be helpful. She just wanted the next eight months to go by quickly with her playing her usual role as an unnamed background character.

"We're going to watch a new show on Netflix, a baking show. Do you girls want to join us?" Aunt Mary asked after their lunches were safely stored.

"I have spreads to look over," Penny said.

"I think I'm going to go read for a bit," Misti said. Penny mouthed "good choice" to her. Uncle Bill looked about ready to fall asleep.

"Okay, just remember, lights out at 10."

Misti followed her cousin up to their rooms.

"Is it okay if I shower?" Misti asked before Penny closed her door.

"Of course; it's your shower too. I prefer to shower in the morning. Are you a night showerer? Dad is. He says it helps him relax."

"I guess," Misti said. She didn't want to tell her that in the past she had to shower whenever she could. There was never really a schedule.

"That's terrific! We don't have to fight over the bathroom! I have to be honest, I was worried about that. Silly of me but, like, I am not a morning person!" Penny came back out into the hallway and opened a closet in the bathroom, getting out two towels.

"You can use my shampoo and conditioner. They have coconut oil and remind me of the beach! Supposed to be good for waves."

21

Penny had straight-as-a-board hair. But Misti was intrigued. She had a natural wave that some girls had told her was nice and even envied.

"Thanks."

Penny grinned.

"I mean, thanks for everything. For being so nice. I realize having me here is an inconvenience. But I promise it is just until after high school." Misti blurted it all out.

Penny stared at her, her eyebrows raised. "You're not an inconvenience, Misti. We absolutely wanted you here once we heard about what had happened. My mom cried, and I overheard her telling my dad that we should have tried to take you years ago." Penny crossed her arms and glanced behind her, checking for the prying ears of her parents. "I don't know if you remember coming here, like, maybe ten years ago?" Misti nodded. The princess party flashed through her mind again. "I remember you and I had so much fun for, like, two weeks. It was summertime, and we had a pool out back and we rode bikes. We stayed up in my room reading scary stories. It was like having a sister!"

Misti felt herself smile genuinely for the first time.

"I woke up one morning and you were gone. I guess your mom just packed up and took you and left in the middle of the night. No goodbyes. It was the first time I saw my mom cry."

Disappearing in the middle of the night was not something unusual to Misti either.

"I'm sorry," Misti apologized. Not that it was her crime. But she had spent her life atoning for her mother.

"It's not your fault," Penny said. "I just know that my mom was worried about you then. And I think she has regretted not trying to find you earlier."

Misti's throat tightened. She had assumed, had been informed by her mother, that they were alone in this world. She did remember leaving that night. She recalled crying in the back of a taxi. And her mother telling her it was better, that her aunt was an evil witch who was going to boil her alive if they stayed. That her aunt was resentful of how pretty Misti was compared to Penny.

"Go shower!" Penny said. "Just unwind. The high school hasn't had a new student in two years. You'll be the star of the show tomorrow!"

A different kind of anxiety gripped Misti's heart.

Misti showered, loving the warm water and taking a deep whiff of the shampoo. It smelled like the beach. Misti thought about the few weeks she and her mom camped on the beach when she was in middle school. It was one of the few good memories she had.

She brushed her hair and dressed in the pjs she had grabbed from her room. When she emerged, Penny's door was ajar. Misti peeked in and saw her on the computer, her eyebrows scrunched together.

Misti went to her room and discovered a couple shirts and a pair of jeans lying on the bed.

"Thought you might prefer something fresh for your new school," the note read, signed "Penny."

The shirts were nothing special. One was a simple T-shirt with stripes. The other was a sweater with a cable knit pattern. The sweater was not long enough for Misti's comfort so she chose the T-shirt. The jeans were newer, never even worn. They had fashionable tears in them and a slight roll at the ankle.

Misti had just finished pulling on the clothes when there was a gentle tap at the door. Misti opened it and Penny grinned.

"I hope you don't mind, but I always prefer having a brand new outfit to wear to school on my first day! You know, the first impression is what counts! You look so cute!"

"Thanks!" Misti wanted to appear displeased that her cousin had deemed her clothes not good enough, but she was glad that she had.

"I have just the thing to finish that off!" Penny skipped back to her room and appeared with a cranberry-colored sweater. Misti put it on.

"This will look fantastic with your boots!" Penny said, clapping her hands in approval.

"Thanks again," Misti whispered.

"Any time!" Penny said. "I already told Dad we'll need his credit card this weekend. No offense, but you need a new wardrobe."

"None taken." Misti had promised herself that she would not become attached. She was an expert at not becoming attached. But now, the first day, she could feel herself breaking that pledge.

After she had switched back to her pjs and Penny had returned to revising her yearbook, Misti propped her pillows against her bed and took out a battered book from her bag. She opened its crisp pages to the next blank one.

She had started keeping a journal during an eighth grade English class. The teacher had forced them to have one during her class, allowing them ten minutes to scribble in it. She vowed to never read it unless they had requested, assuring them that their lives would be better if they got their feelings out on paper. Misti had been uncertain initially, just writing out song lyrics. One day, she opened up with little events and then moved on to bigger moments: her concerns about her mom, her latest living condition. And although she moved after being at that school for only six weeks, she had continued with the journaling.

Dear J,

(The teacher had told them they should name their journals, like Anne Frank had. Misti hadn't been able to think of anything and didn't like the idea of naming it something you would a pet, so just put "J" instead of "dear journal.")

I've been thinking about what that social worker said, about taking time to make this a new, fresh start. I think I'm going to do that. Penny isn't as horrible as I expected. And Aunt Mary and Uncle Bill are nice. But it is the first day. New always seems better on the first day. We will see how it really is after a few weeks. They might get over having a permanent guest.

Misti stopped writing, biting the inside of her lip, her chest tightening again.

Penny told me I would be the star of the show tomorrow. I really hope not. At least she gave me some new clothes so I don't look like the slob I usually do. Do you think I should stop wearing eyeliner? I didn't put it back on today and I kind of liked it. That can be part of the new appearance. Mom always said eyeliner was a warning. It scared the right people. But, all things considered, Mom isn't the best person to think about right now. You know I don't like to talk about it. Nervous for tomorrow. But, overall, things aren't as bad as I was expecting.

Four

First Day

The morning went smoothly. Penny was not a morning person and took a long time to get ready. Misti had not slept well. Normally, she knew that she would be leaving in a few months and it didn't particularly matter if she made a good first impression. But this situation was different. She was in this school for the rest of the year. And her cousin was going there. She didn't want to be an embarrassment. She had thought about all of this while completing a very minimal makeup look and dressing in her borrowed clothes. Aunt Mary must have known that Penny had given her clothes because she smiled at her daughter with approval before they all headed out. Uncle Bill left in his truck, Penny left in her Camry, and Misti and Mary drove off in the SUV.

"Are you nervous?" Aunt Mary asked after she parked. Kids were streaming into the building, some by themselves, some with a single companion, others in packs. Misti's heart was racing but she shook her head. No need to worry her aunt.

The enrollment process was mostly complete when they entered.

Misti's grades had been transferred, and judging by the sad look the counselor gave her along with a comforting pat on her forearm, Misti knew she had been told about her past. The counselor was an older woman attempting to look ten years younger. Her hair was cut in a long bob and she wore a thick layer of makeup with bright eyeliner. She kept pushing up jangling bracelets only for them to fall back to her wrist and clink like Christmas bells as she typed.

"Okay, Misti, here are your classes. It looks like you have all your credits except English and a couple electives. Now you have your choice of electives: We have Drama, Choir, Band, Art, Creative Writing, Gym, Weight Lifting, and TA." Bracelets shoved back up her arm. "I'm going to put you in senior English with Ms. Williams for the first hour. After that, you can have your choice." Bracelets clinked.

Misti selected Art for her first elective. The thought of getting on stage and performing terrified her, and she was not musically inclined. Instead she picked creative writing. She did like writing in her journal. Probably something she could force her way through.

The rest of her schedule was filled with a Statistics and Financial Planning class, and a study hall. Not a horrible schedule.

"Okay, well, I guess that's all," Aunt Mary stood with them. "Are you ready for this?"

Misti nodded, afraid the nervousness she was trying to hide would reveal itself if she spoke. Strong and silent. That was her strategy for the next eight months.

"Okay, Penny will bring you home. I'll be home at about the same time as both of you." Aunt Mary stared at her for a moment and looked at the wacky counselor before grabbing Misti, hugging her, then bolting away.

Misti was given a map of the school and a code to a locker. Then she was set free.

The first bell had not yet rung, but Misti thought it would be wise to find her first class and get her bearings. On her way down the wide hall, she noticed people stopping and turning from their lockers, looking at her with gaping mouths and popping gum. A few boys pushed each other and a couple girls looked her up and down. She was pleased to see that she was dressed a lot like them today. It would be easy to blend in.

"Misti!" Penny appeared beside her. "Let me see your schedule." She snatched the schedule from her hands and they kept walking. "Misti, this is my best friend Chloe." Penny was carrying a coffee, something she did not have before she left that morning.

"Nice to meet you!" Chloe said. She was a short girl with black hair and small eyes that seemed to dart. Misti did not like her. Her eyes held no trust.

"We don't have any classes together but you have a sweet schedule. All of your teachers are actually decent at their jobs." Penny handed back her schedule. "Your English teacher is the best one in the building. She's older but definitely understanding." Penny was leading the way, pretending to ignore but actually loving the eyes on her as she escorted the new girl.

"She's just down the hall from my class." She pointed at a door that had a sign leaning against it. "Your second and third hours are close to mine too; I can come get you. After the third hour, we'll find your locker and then go to lunch." Misti was relieved that Penny was taking charge of the situation. She would not have to interact with anyone new. "See you in a bit!"

Misti walked to the room alone and found the sign read: "I don't have bad handwriting, I'm just using my own font!" Misti liked Ms. Williams immediately.

"Hello! You must be my new student!" The teacher rose from her desk. She was wearing a full-length skirt and boots with a loose peasant blouse. She reminded Misti of the hippie woman who had read to her after school when she was little when her mom was working, back when her mom could manage a full-time job.

"I am. I just wanted to find the class before being late," Misti explained.

"Responsible, I like it!" The teacher moved to the front of the room and took a book from the shelf. "We're reading this in class. We just started a few days ago. Today is a writing prompt over the first ten chapters. You can just get caught up."

Misti nodded and looked at the book. *To Kill a Mockingbird.* She had actually already read it, but she chose not to say anything. It had been a few years and she would like the chance to read it again before making a fool of herself.

"I have no seating chart, but my students kind of assign themselves seats. There are a few open in the middle of that row. Yes, right there is good." Misti settled into the desk and opened the book. She was halfway through chapter one when the bell rang and other students started coming in.

Most students just stared at her. She heard a few whispers but did not look up to acknowledge them.

"We do have a new student, and yes, she is pretty, boys, and yes, girls, she is smart. Just leave her alone and get out some paper. You have a writing prompt." There was a groan but everyone listened and soon the class had pulled their attention away from Misti and to their assignment.

The next two classes went about the same. Her math teacher gave her a packet, asking her to complete it by Friday, and she took notes over the day's lesson. The creative writing class was sharing stories and her teacher told her she would jump in on the next assignment. Misti listened to some pretty horribly written stories about teenage girl troubles. By the end of the third hour, Misti was ready to go home. The lack of sleep the night before and the nerves had caught up to her.

She was feeling overwhelmed and behind.

"Locker time!" Penny said in her mother's sing-song voice. Misti held out her locker card and Penny paused, frowning.

"What?" Misti asked.

"Nothing, just...there are some weird stories about that locker. They don't usually let kids have it."

Great. Now she had the weird locker.

"What stories?"

"Uh, just weird ones. I guess a girl who had this locker, like, twenty years ago died or something and people say it's haunted."

A ghost locker. That seemed highly unlikely. And something Misti would be stuck with.

"I know, I know. But we're a small town; people are silly!"

They found the locker. It was in between one locker that was covered in bumper stickers about saving the planet and another that looked as if it had been punched a couple too many times. Misti did the twirls of the code and the locker popped open. It was dusty inside. It was clear no one had used it in quite a while. Misti deposited her bag, taking with her only her lunch and the copy of her code. Penny assured her they would have time to come back before the fourth hour.

Lunch provided Misti with a little recovery. She half listened to Penny and Chloe discuss yearbook issues—everything from what to put on something they kept referring to as the 'fun spread' to how so and so was not doing her share again and that Mr. Miller was doing literally nothing about it and it was so freaking annoying. While she listened, Misti ate her sandwich and people-watched. She was still being looked at and whispered about. The school was a lot smaller than any she had attended before. She was able to recognize kids from her classes. There was a slender kid with baggy pants and a shirt for a heavy metal band who was in her English and her math class.There was the girl who was in her creative writing class with red curly hair, a baggy sweater, and a large book she had her nose buried in.

There were the typical tables that all schools held. There was the loud, needing-to-make-themselves-noticed-and-heard sports boys table. Close by was the cheerleading table, not really eating much and taking lots of selfies. There was a quiet table with kids eating their lunch in an attempt to be invisible. Book girl was there. There was a table with the band kids. Heavy metal was there.

Misti placed herself at the in-between table. They were not as socially outcast as the quiet table and not as in the center of it as the sports and cheerleaders. She was okay with her positioning. Normally, she had eaten lunch in the library or outside away from the noise. When she could afford lunch, that is. Most of the time, she just sat and did the homework she had gotten in her morning classes, away from the danger of the cafeteria.

"Hey, Penny." A tall boy in an Under Armour hoodie and jeans stopped by their table. He held an apple and looked like a cliché jock wanna be. He wasn't particularly attractive. He wasn't out of shape but you could tell he wasn't really in shape either. His hair had too much gel in it and his smile looked painted on. He did have nice, straight, white teeth that seemed to gleam at them.

"Hi, Tony!" Penny instantly perked up, tossing her hair.

"How's it going?" His eyes traveled over the three girls, lingering on Misti for a moment. Misti took a bite of her sandwich, uninterested in his attention.

"Just talking yearbook shop!" Penny said, glancing at Misti. "This is my cousin, Misti. She just moved here. She's staying with me, actually." Penny had changed. She was no longer the take-charge, in-control girl who had firmly led Misti from class to class today. Instead she was this high-pitched voice, nervous creature. Misti stared at her, confused for a moment.

"Nice to meet you. I'm Tony. I'm on the football team and basketball team. Backup quarterback." He puffed his chest in pride. All Misti heard was "not good enough to be the original quarterback."

"Cool," Misti said, deciding it would be better to be nice. She was, after all, trying to create a fresh new start.

"You guys coming to the game Friday night?"

Sports? Misti had never attended a sports event in her life. The closest was when she watched people play football or soccer in the park. And she didn't really understand the point in those slow-motion versions.

"You know it!" Penny said before giggling. Chloe joined in but Misti did not.

"Cool. I'll look for you guys." He winked at Penny and walked away. "Oh, my God!" Penny's voice hit a new decibel and she and Chloe squealed at each other a little. "I can't even believe I just acted like that! I mean, I must have sounded like an idiot!"

"At least he finally asked you to the game!" Chloe said. Did he, though? Misti wanted to know how him asking if they were going meant he was asking Penny.

"I know! I've only been dropping hints all year!"

Misti was lost now. She herself had never been interested in a boy, so maybe this was normal behavior. She turned her attention to the tables of the sports boys and the cheerleaders. Lunch had been eaten and the boys and girls were now mingling. She saw many girls giggling while most of the boys appeared to be acting foolishly, hitting each other and using trays as bats for empty milk cartons. Misti had never paid attention to high school behavior before. Maybe she was the weird one.

"We should go to our lockers." Confident Penny returned, taking control and speaking at a pleasant level. Misti zipped her lunch bag up and the three girls walked to their lockers. Misti opened hers and placed her lunch inside, grabbing her bag. She would have to bring something to wipe it out with tomorrow. The dust was all over her bag now.

Misti's last class of the day was Art. This was her favorite class. The teacher was a quiet, short man with glasses and no hair. He gave Misti a tour of the studio before giving her paper and charcoal.

"We are experimenting with this medium currently. You are required to draw something, anything, with the charcoal before you can move onto what you like." Misti nodded and took a seat at an empty table. The class was not full. Music was playing in the background. Misti recognized most of the kids from her other classes. The stares of shock at the new student had passed and a few of the kids actually smiled at her.

Misti stared at the paper for a long time, wondering what she should draw. Soon, she just let her mind go and began to doodle.

"Not bad!" Mr. Wilson said. "You're talented!"

The picture was a cluster of trees, all dead, in a bunched pattern She had added a moon and was considering a lake in the right bottom corner, possibly with a monster emerging from it.

At the end of the class Mr. Wilson said, "You can keep this with you, or we have cubbies over there. The artists here are all very respectful of each other's pieces."

Misti found an empty cubbie and put the paper in upside down.

She found her way back to her locker and opened it. She was surprised to find it was no longer dirty. In fact, it looked brand new. Penny had probably alerted a custodian and asked for it to be cleaned while she was in class.

Misti retrieved her lunch pail, the book for English, and her math packet. No other class had given homework tonight.

"You ready?" Penny appeared next to her.

Penny was not a horrible driver, but Misti found herself gripping the sides of her seats a few times as they rolled through some stop signs in front of cars that were going a lot faster than they should have been.

"What do you mean, you don't know how to drive?" Penny asked. She had to shout to be heard over the music that she had blasting. The car was an older model but Penny had made it her own. It smelled like strawberries and she had put on seat covers with a red pattern. The car was just as clean as her room, with the exception of their bags tumbling around the back seat.

"Didn't really have to know in the city. Besides, we never had a car."

"Oh, right! That makes sense. I'm sorry. That was probably insensitive of me."

Misti forgave her. In fact, Misti had always wanted to learn to drive. Most of her classmates knew how to. But they didn't have a car when she turned sixteen, and her mother had not driven in years herself.

They arrived home in one piece and found themselves alone in the house. Misti followed Penny up the steps of the drive. They hung their jackets and bags on the hooks, removed their shoes, and walked to the kitchen. Penny had begun explaining yearbook terms to Misti.

"When I say 'spread' I actually mean two pages, but yearbook calls it 'the spread'. We also have the mugshots, which are just everyone's picture. But it's hilarious because we call them that. Right now we're finishing up the fall spreads and then we'll be moving on to the mugs. Those are always the easiest." Penny pulled down a snack from the pantry and began eating and continued talking. Misti let her. She knew what is was like to be lonely and want to speak.

After they had each had a snack, they headed up to their rooms. Misti sat on her bed and worked on the packet. It seemed to be pretty basic algebra. She was about halfway through when there was a tap on her door. Misti waited for it to open before realizing the person was waiting for her response.

"Come in!" She had never had that control before. It was pretty exciting.

Aunt Mary entered. She was dressed in slacks and a silky blouse with flowers all over it. Her hair was done up and she wore stockings.

"How was your first day?" she asked, coming to sit on the edge of the bed.

"Good. Pretty easy. Penny really helped me, made sure I got to all of my classes."

Aunt Mary smiled. "I see you have homework."

"Yeah, not much," Misti said, showing her the packet. "Personal finance."

"Well, lucky for you, I deal with these sorts of things all day, everyday. So if you need any help, you let me know. Lord knows I can't do what Penny is taking." Aunt Mary stood. "Better get dinner started. Spaghetti tonight!"

Aunt Mary shut the door behind her. Privacy. Again. Misti didn't know how to handle that.

Dinner followed the same routine as the night before. Uncle Bill also asked about their days and Penny complained about Mr. Miller and told them about almost being done with yearbook. Misti just said she had a good day and that her teachers seemed okay.

After dinner, the girls did the dishes and made their lunches. Misti went upstairs after dinner and took another shower. Penny did not leave another outfit for her this time but Misti had paid attention to what the girls were wearing and managed to put together what she thought would be acceptable. She got into bed and read more of the book for English.

"Lights out, girls!" Aunt Mary called up the stairs right at 10.

Misti could get used to this life.

Five

The Game

The week flew by. Misti was able to participate more fully in her classes. By Friday, she could find her classes without having to ask or circle back. She got her first creative writing assignment and finished her monster in the lake charcoal drawing, which Mr. Wilson described as inspired and hung up with other student work.

She was drawing random circles in her book when she felt as if she was being watched. She looked up and found a boy staring at her from across the Art room. When she looked at him, he looked away. He was still working on his charcoal piece. He wore dark jeans and a plain T-shirt. Misti would classify him as cute. When the bell rang, she hurried out the door to avoid meeting him.

Misti opened her locker and froze. Everything in it had been moved from where she had set it. Her lunch pail, which she always set on the bottom, was hanging from the hook, slightly open. Her books that she kept in a stack in order of her classes were all piled on the bottom of the locker on top of her jacket, which usually hung where the lunch pail was now. Misti's eyebrows furrowed in annoyance. She must not have shut her locker and now some jerk was messing with the new girl. As she rearranged her things, she remembered what Penny had said on the first day: that she had the haunted locker.

Someone was trying to convince her that the locker was haunted. Trying to scare her. She looked around, but the halls were relatively empty. No one was obviously watching her, hoping for a reaction. Tears? Fear? She wouldn't give them the satisfaction. And after what she had been through, it would take more than a few moved items to give her the creeps.

"See you next week!" She closed the door firmly and twisted the lock a few times, ensuring it was shut. She picked up her bag full of her weekend assignments and went to meet Penny at the car, looking back only once to scan the hall for a suspect. No one was left.

Misti was sitting at the island, searching the internet and eating a snack, when Penny came thundering down the stairs.

"Here!" Penny slid a blue shirt across the island to her and went to the counter. "You'll need a school shirt tonight. You have to wear school colors to show your support." She picked up an apple.

"Uh," Misti said, holding up the shirt. It had a tiger on it and in yellow font said 'Blackwood High'. "I don't know if football games are really my thing."

"Oh, come on! You told me you've never even been to one. How can you know if they're your thing or not?"

That was one of the more solid arguments that Penny had given over the past few days. And Misti reminded herself that she was trying to be a new person.

The game was packed. There were parents and students and small children running around. The air was cold; Misti was glad Aunt Mary had tossed her a pair of gloves and headband for her ears. Penny had redone her hair and applied a bit more makeup than usual. They had picked up Chloe and they both had cameras. They were covering the game; a girl named Angela was supposed to, but she backed out last minute and this was the third most important game of the season so it needed to be covered.

Misti trailed behind the two girls and regretted coming. The mountain air had a bite to it and the crowd made her uncomfortable. The three made their way down the old wooden bleachers to sit with a growing crowd of teenagers. In the front of the group were eight skinny boys. They had no shirts on but they were painted in blue and yellow, the school colors. They each had a letter on their chests and stomachs; when they stood in the correct order they spelled out "GO TIGERS." Most of the time, they could not find the "O" and the "T" kept sitting down. The cheerleaders down below were yelling and waving up at the stands.

The energy in the stands was different from anything Misti had ever experienced. It buzzed inside her, as if there was a bumble bee rumbling around her chest. The hairs on her arms rose in excitement and she actually joined in the cheering when the football team ran through the banner the cheerleaders held out for them. Misti clapped, but everyone around her thundered. A senior girl sang the national anthem that sent the crowd into a frenzy. She held the last note long but no one seemed to be bothered. The band beat their drums feverishly in support and Misti saw the girl rejoined them to her own cheers. She picked up a saxophone blushing as they all gushed about how well she had done.

Misti asked Penny about Tony and learned that he was number 12. They found him standing away from everyone else, his hands around his collar, swaying from side to side. He looked smaller than the other players.

The game began and the cheering rose again to an almost deafening level. Misti wondered if it would be bad form to cover her ears. Penny and Chloe were jumping around with the crowd, pausing to snap pictures of the band, the kick-off, and the crowd. Every ten minutes or so, the cheerleaders would lead the crowd in a cheer. Misti discovered that everyone around her knew exactly how to respond to the questions the cheerleaders asked. At one point, she was forced to link arms with Penny and a girl next to her and they hopped left and right, simply shouting the colors of their school.

None of it helped their team. The other team scored, then scored again.

Throughout the game, Penny and Chloe whispered about Tony. Misti didn't ask why Penny was obsessed with the one guy who never played, who was always standing just outside the huddle, who didn't seem to be talking to anyone on the team. Misti almost felt bad for Tony.

"I'm going to go get some hot chocolate," Misti said to Penny, who was busy snapping pictures of the crowd. Uncle Bill had slipped Misti a ten before they headed out the door. "Do you want anything?"

"No, I'm good." Penny didn't look up. She was examining the pictures on her camera.

Misti clambered out of the stands and made her way up to the top of the bleachers and over to a little shack. There was a small group around it but no one was in line. Misti came to the front and recognized the girl behind the counter from her Art class.

"Misti, right?" the girl asked. Her name was Amber, Misti thought, giving her a nod. "Cool! Glad you're joining in the school spirit already! What can I get you?" Maybe coming to the game wasn't the worst idea after all.

"Hot chocolate?"

"Coming right up!" Amber turned and pulled out the coffee cups.

"How are you liking it here?"

"It's pretty nice. A lot different than where I was before. A lot smaller."

"Man, I wish I had lived in a big city. There's, like, nothing to do here but come to the games and then go to the stupid drive-in after. Can't wait to get out of here!"

Misti nodded. She had heard that sentiment a lot over the last four days. She wanted to tell her classmates that they should enjoy it here because the big city was not as glamorous as the TV shows made it sound. But she doubted they would listen to the new girl. And although she had spent most of her life in different cities, she always spent them in the slums, not the nice parts. Maybe the nice parts of cities were better. "That will be a dollar!"

Misti handed over the ten and got a five and five ones back. She thought about telling the girl, but she didn't know if that would embarrass her. She thanked her for the (free) hot chocolate and headed back down. She stopped at the top of the bleachers, taking a sip and immediately regretting it. The liquid was lava hot, burning her tongue. She winced, knowing now every sip would have little to no flavor. At least it was free.

"They should warn you not to drink those for at least ten minutes after getting them; they always burn your mouth." Misti turned and found the boy she saw in art class today staring back at her. He was just as attractive up close. He was tall, a lot taller than she had thought, with a lean but not skinny body. He was wearing a hoodie and a beanie with a fuzzy ball on top. He had his hands shoved in his pocket and a slight smile on his lips. His eyes were green and his hair black.

"Yeah." Misti could not think of anything else to say.

"I'm Alex. We have art together."

She nodded, looking at her cup of hot chocolate. They stood together in awkward silence, watching the events of the game with little interest.

40

The crowd in the stand began to chant. One last rally for their team.

"They're down 24 to 0. I really don't think chanting is going to help," Alex said, breaking the ever-growing silence.

"I've never actually been to a game before. It's odd the amount of support they have for a team that's not doing what they're supposed to do," Misti said. She sounded dumb and pretentious.

Alex nodded. He must be one of the ones who liked to cheer. "I saw your charcoal drawing in Art. You're really talented."

"Thanks." Misti would have blushed if her cheeks weren't already red from cold. No one ever noticed what she did.

"I'm not much of an artist. I just took the class to fill my schedule and my friend said that anyone can learn to do it. I'm not sure."

"Maybe I can help you," Misti heard herself say before she could check in with herself. What was she thinking? Helping this guy? Why?

"That would be great!" Alex grinned at her and Misti's stomach did a little backflip. That was new and different. She now understood why her cousin had been acting like such an idiot every time Tony spoke to her. It was involuntary.

"There you are!" A voice interrupted their conversation. A short girl with a pixie cut appeared next to them. Her blue eyes were covered in dark eyeliner, similar to what Misti used to wear, and she had several piercings, including her eyebrows, nose, and ears. Misti's stomach mislanded and she felt a pang. This was why she had never let herself be interested in boys. Because they always had an angle, always had other interests, other girls. She had seen it with her mother's slew of boyfriends. And this cute boy, the one who noticed her, already had a girl.

"I should get back to my cousin. See you in Art." She turned and hurried back to Penny and Chloe before he could introduce her, explain her away as a cousin. She was relieved, actually. If he already had a girl, then she had nothing to worry about. His intentions might really just be about learning art.

"Where have you been?" Penny asked. She looked concerned.

"Some guy from Art class was talking to me."

"Ohh!" Chloe said.

"He just wants help with his stuff," Misti said, shaking her head. "Pretty sure he had a girlfriend."

"Who is it?"

"Some kid named Alex. Don't know his last name."

Penny shrugged, looking around for him. Misti glanced to where they had been standing but he was gone. Off to make out with his edgy girlfriend.

They only stayed ten more minutes before Penny decided they needed to beat the crowd and get to the drive-in before everyone else. As Chloe and Penny discussed the game and how horrible the refs were, a complaint that the game could not possibly be the team's fault, Misti thought about her last few days and the 'new' version of herself. She was clearly liked; people she had not spoken to before were chatting with her at the game. But the new version of herself had let emotions come in and that was not okay. She could see herself coming to care for her aunt and uncle and Penny. But they were family, and they had already done more than they needed to. As for the rest of these kids, she had no desire to get involved or emotionally invested in any of them. Especially any boys. Because boys will derail your plans and make life messy.

Within ten minutes of their arrival and ordering of ice cream shakes, the rest of the drive-in was full of cars. One car rolled up and began to play loud music. Everyone else moved from car to car, again, discussing the unfairness of the refs. Misti watched and listened, slowly consuming her chocolate shake. After about thirty minutes, the football team arrived. They acted as if they had just won the Superbowl.

For about an hour, the poor workers ran from building to car, wiggling in between teenagers who stood in the way, looking annoyed when they were told to get back into their cars by management.

"Is it always like this?" Misti asked Chloe and Penny.

"Always. At least there hasn't been a fight yet," Chloe replied.

"If this night didn't pay all of their bills, I'm sure they wouldn't let us come here," Penny said, pressing her lips together as two girls ran by giggling fiercely as a couple football players gave chase, throwing ice cubes at them.

Misti was ready for bed, but she said nothing. Penny was on edge, looking around, scanning frantically for Tony. They waited for another thirty minutes before he arrived. Misti had missed part of the game during her hot chocolate adventure. From what she did watch, Tony had not played at all during this game. But the way he was acting he alone played every single minute.

"Hey girls!" he said, his smile oozing across his face. "Did you enjoy the game?"

Misti's feeling of empathy was gone the second he opened his mouth.

"Oh, sure! Would have been better if we'd had some fair refs!"

"For sure, for sure. We'll do better next week."

Misti doubted that and must have rolled her eyes out loud because Tony looked at her. "What did you think of the game, gorgeous?" he asked her.

Misti saw those words punch Penny in the stomach. She needed to save this situation. And she was just cranky enough to do that. "Your team sucks."

Chloe looked at her, mouth hanging open in awe. Penny looked over her shoulder at her, her eyes afire. Tony was clearly annoyed. "Do you know anything about football?"

"Nope. But I know that if you lose with no points, it can't be all the refs' fault."

There was nothing but the laughter from the other cars and the music breaking the silence. Misti might have gone too far, but she just wanted Penny to know she had no interest in this guy. She also wanted Penny to stop throwing herself at him. He was a douche.

"Do you want to see some of the shots we got for the yearbook?" Chloe asked.

"Sure!" Tony turned his little eyes away from Misti. The three ignored Misti for the next thirty minutes. Penny had returned to her usual high-pitched voice and giggle that she assumed whenever she spoke with Tony. To her surprise, Chloe also seemed to be flirting with Tony. Penny didn't seem to notice—or maybe this was some plan they had. Maybe this is what best friends did: Flirt with your crush to get them to like you more? Maybe Misti should have giggled and looked away when he called her gorgeous. Maybe that would have helped Penny.

Misti looked at her phone, another gift from her aunt and uncle. It was close to midnight now. Her uncle had been pretty clear about being home no later than then. Plus the lights were starting to go out and other cars were leaving.

"There's a party happening at Joey's place," Tony said. "You two want to come?" Misti was not included in that invitation. Maybe she should look hurt.

"Sure!" Chloe said as Penny said "I can't." The two friends looked at each other.

"I have a curfew," Penny said. "Maybe next time."

Tony nodded and said goodnight before heading back to his car.

"We could go just once!" Chloe was saying.

"There's drinking at those parties! And I've heard they are starting to do drugs now too," Penny said. "I'm not interested in doing that."

"We have to live a little while we're in school! Before we get too old and start having kids!"

Penny laughed and shook her head. "How soon are you having those?"

Chloe shrugged and pouted all the way home. They dropped her off and Misti climbed into the front seat. The drive was silent other than the road singing to them.

"You didn't have to be so mean to Tony," Penny said as they turned down their road. "He's not the star of the team, but he's a really good guy. He's just lost between being a football guy and being a good guy." Misti didn't think you could be lost between those. And she was angry with her cousin for defending him. Penny must realize that Tony was not a good guy. She just really wanted him to be one. And Misti knew from watching her mother that guys don't change.

Uncle Bill was waiting for them. The TV was on ESPN.

"11:58!" he said, standing from the couch. "Cutting it close, ladies."

"Oh, Dad!" Penny rolled her eyes. "Some people would let their daughter who is almost eighteen be out as late as they want."

"Those people are raising their own grandchildren," Uncle Bill said so drily back that Misti actually laughed. Uncle Bill perked up. Misti had not laughed since living with them.

Penny rolled her eyes again. "Good night, Daddy," she said, heading up the stairs. Misti pulled out the ten dollars from her pocket and tried giving it back to her uncle.

"You keep it. Payment for laughing at my joke. No one ever does! Also, I understand you're going on a shopping adventure tomorrow."

Misti had forgotten about that. Hopefully, Penny would not be mad at her by then.

Six

The Shift

The next morning, Misti woke later than she meant. She came down the stairs just after 10, expecting to find the household in a bustle, but it was calm. She could hear her feet padding on the carpet as she walked into the living room. She found Aunt Mary watching TV, savoring a mug of coffee.

"Morning! How was the game?"

"Okay. They lost." Misti sat on the sectional.

"They ordinarily do. We need a different coach. But we can't get one until this old fart retires. He's been around so long, no one wants to get rid of him."

Misti found it fascinating that everyone said "we," regardless of their status of being on the team or even attending the school.

"Seems silly if he isn't good at his job anymore."

"Small town politics." Aunt Mary shrugged. "Penny will sleep in until noon, no doubt. I'm sure she was up late chatting to Chloe on her phone about whatever boy interests they have right now." There was a pause. Misti knew she had already upset her cousin once last

46

night. She didn't desire to add to that by informing her aunt about Tony. "Anyhow, after she wakes up, we could take a girls' day and run up to the city—get you some new clothes if you like."

Misti had never had the privilege of going to the city to get new clothes. Her wardrobe comprised either used or very used clothes. But she didn't want to receive handouts. As if reading the conflict on her face, Aunt Mary smiled.

"Think of it like all the missed Christmas and birthday presents for the previous seventeen years."

Misti blushed and looked down. "I would like that."

"Perfect! Better eat breakfast. Try not to make too much noise. Your uncle gets to sleep in on the weekends and he does so." Mary rolled her eyes.

Misti filled her cereal bowl and was munching quietly at the bar when the phone rang.

"Damn!" Mary rushed up and snatched the phone. "Hello...oh, yes, hello." Mary glanced over at Misti and turned her back, hunching her shoulders. It was about her. Probably the social worker. It had been just over five days since Misti arrived. Checking in. "Yes, yes, doing just lovely. We're going shopping today. Hm? Oh. Well, yes. I haven't told her yet. I will. I'll get the appointment set up for next week."Appointment. Misti swirled her spoon around in her cereal, suddenly not starving but too poor to know it was bad form to waste food.

"Thank you, goodbye." Mary hung up the phone and took a moment to swing around.

"What did she need?"

The social worker was a young up-and-comer. She was by the book and Misti had found her to be overbearing and lacking the empathy that a social worker should have. She liked to talk down to people. She did it to everybody, her aunt included.

"You're supposed to start therapy. You were expected to start this week. But I felt you would prefer to be in school first, get settled and then start."

"I would. I'm glad I got to do that." Misti wanted her aunt to know that she didn't think she had done anything wrong.

"Well, we'll try to get you scheduled so you don't have to miss school. Is there a day you would prefer?"

Misti shook her head. Talking to someone about her feelings was not something she loved to do. And she did not want to talk about that day. It was awful enough that it happened. No amount of talking would change that. But if it meant Social Worker Sally left her aunt alone, she could go suffer through an hour every once in a while.

"All right. I'll take care of it on Monday."

"I'm sorry." Misti apologized mostly out of nature, but she didn't know what to say.

"Oh, dear. There's nothing to be sorry for!" Aunt Mary reached over and patted her hand. "That woman just has a way of making anyone she speaks to feel like a moron and a child all at the same time. Here I thought I was doing a satisfactory job of getting you adjusted."

"You are!" Misti said. "I had never been to a football game before last night." Misti stopped herself from revealing all the new things she had never had before, like eating three meals in one day. Or coming back to a tidy home where no one was lying passed out on the sofa. But she guessed if she couldn't handle social workers, she couldn't deal with hearing about that. Aunt Mary looked horrified enough that that had been her first football game.

Misti forced herself to finish breakfast and fled upstairs to get ready for shopping. She took a long shower, reflecting on the last week. She recognized she had been so busy working to get caught up in all of her classes (her math teacher had looked stunned when she turned the packet back into him, done on Friday) that she was exhausted. After her shower, she let her hair air dry, and she sat down to write an update to J.

Dear J,

Things are going pretty well so far. The school is not bad. I've definitely been in worse. I really like my art class. The instructor seems to know what he is doing. I don't mind any of my teachers, really. Penny is cool. It is pretty nifty having someone my own age to relate to. She is probably mad at me still. I thought I could do better, but this guy Tony is just no good. He seems like he wants to be more than he is and Penny deserves someone who is already more. If that makes sense. I hope she gets over him soon before he hurts her.

Aunt Mary and Penny are taking me shopping today. I was torn, but getting to buy new clothes will be a real treat. I'll be sure to keep it under control.

I'm thinking about seeing if Uncle Bill and Aunt Mary will let me get a job.

I have to start therapy next week. Like I will tell anyone outside of these pages what really happened that day. It isn't like it will change anything. What is done is done. Did I miss something that could have prevented it? Probably. But will talking about it really help? Doubtful.

Misti went back downstairs and found Uncle Bill watching football.

She sat down with him, offering him a "morning." He grunted back at her. Penny woke thirty minutes later. Misti heard the shower turn on. When she arrived downstairs, her hair was done and she was dressed as if she was going to school.

"All right, girls, we leave in twenty minutes!" Aunt Mary had joined the football party, wearing a college team jersey and jeans, her hair pulled into a pony and wearing comfy tennis shoes.

"I actually can't go." Penny said, moving to the fridge. "A bunch of spreads need to be edited, and a bunch didn't even get done. I was going to go over to Chloe's so we could get those finished."

There was a pause. Aunt Mary glanced at Misti and then Penny, pursing her lips.

"What?" Penny said, teenage attitude signing through. Uncle Bill sat up and glowered at his daughter and she turned away, averting his frown.

"It's okay," Misti said. "She told me last night that she might not go. Angela didn't do what she was supposed to, I guess?"

Penny stared at Misti. For a moment, she looked as if she might change her mind. The ice was thawing.

"Yeah."

Aunt Mary relaxed.

"You do what you have to, dear. We'll miss you."

Penny nodded, leaving the room. They heard the door open and shut a few minutes later.

So, she was mad. Great. So much for making things better here.

Shopping was more entertaining than Misti was expecting. She had grown up seeing people wander around with their bags. Her mother told her that people who went shopping were just seeking to fill empty parts in their souls. Once again, her mother had been incorrect. She had set a budget for herself, but she and her aunt walked into a clearance sale. Misti ended up coming home with several bags of clothes containing new shirts, pants, dresses, and shoes. And the prices were what Aunt Mary said was a steal. Aunt Mary had become more comfortable as the day went on, gossiping with Misti about her work and her uncertainties about Penny. She even told her some scandal about a coworker they ran into at lunch.

Penny glanced at them from the couch when they returned and looked put out. Aunt Mary announced their achievement, holding up their bags as if they were trophies. Uncle Bill rolled his eyes, demanding proof. Aunt Mary handed over the receipts and Uncle Bill looked amazed and approving.

"We'll wash this all tomorrow. Take the bags up to your room for now!" Aunt Mary said.

Misti hurried up the stairs, carefully taking everything out and laying it gently on her bed, admiring her new wardrobe.

"You didn't have to cover for me this morning." Penny was leaning against her door, watching her.

"I know. But I get that I upset you."

Misti didn't look at her, just opened her closet and put away her three new sets of shoes. Penny said nothing for a while, looking at the new clothes. She finally turned and walked away. Misti wanted to feel bad for her, but she didn't know how to. She wasn't the one who told her not to go. Penny was being silly. Misti only said those things so Tony would know she was not interested and keep his focus on her cousin, who was so into him it was painful.

The rest of the weekend went by in a blur. Misti watched a college football game with her uncle before her aunt made him turn on a movie. They ordered pizza for dinner and watched another movie after dinner, microwaving popcorn. Penny joined them, but she and Misti did not speak. Misti wondered if her aunt and uncle noticed, but she knew there was no way that they couldn't. Misti would tell them the truth if they asked, but Sunday chore day came and they said nothing.

Misti was in charge of her laundry and vacuuming. She did her chores before returning upstairs to work on her homework, which was almost all done. She wrote a note in her journal, letting him know that her first weekend was a success, other than Penny still being upset with her. She picked out an outfit for the next day as she folded her

51

laundry and returned downstairs, requesting to help in the kitchen. Aunt Mary taught her how to prepare a roast, with carrots and potatoes. It was simple.

Penny drove Misti to school the next morning and said nothing to her. When they arrived, Penny left her in the dust, joining hips with Chloe as they moved up the steps to the school. The safety Misti had felt her first week in that school was dissolving. Penny had been an instant friend, something she had never had before. And now she was alone again. Not like that was super new. Misti sighed.

She went to her locker and prepared for her first few classes. As she approached the locker, Misti had to stop. The combination was spinning. Was it? Maybe? She stepped forward. Yes, it was. Slowly rolling to the right. She looked around to see if there was someone, anyone, to confirm this. No one was around. When she looked back, the lock was still. Misti shook her head and stepped up to the locker, quickly doing the combination and depositing her lunch pail and her afternoon class supplies before slamming the locker and walking away. She was just seeing things. But her stomach was in knots.

Classes went slowly, but more students were talking to her. In English, they paired up to do an activity for the novel and a girl who Misti had determined was fairly smart was her partner. They divided the work and went at it, slowly chatting about things. Her name was Sarah and she, like everyone else she had met, had been born and raised here. She was not in a hurry to go anywhere, except college.

"I'll take over my parents' veterinary shop. So I have to get into a decent school and then vet school." Sarah wrinkled her nose at her perfectly looped handwriting before erasing and rewriting it. "I work there now, part-time. After school and on weekends. I just mostly sit with animals and take phone calls. Do you have a job yet?" Sarah was average height and was a little broad across the shoulders. Her hair was pulled back into a high, tight ponytail and her brown eyes were wide and makeup-free. Her sweater had no logo, and she wore jeans that had no tears and sneakers that looked well-worn but comfortable.

When she was with her mother, Misti had worked at two places for a while. One job was as a clerk at the local corner store and the other involved clearing off tables at the Chinese place they lived above for a few months. She had enjoyed working but never saw much of her money. She had to make sure they paid rent and got some food. It was never enough because she still went to school.

"I haven't looked. My aunt and uncle, they want me to kind of get used to things here first."

"Like there is much to get used to. Just a bunch of old traditions and bad ghost stories."

Misti thought about her locker and the spinning lock.

"What?" Sarah stopped writing and looked at her. "Sorry, I love ghosts and anything paranormal. Weird, I know. But, it is so interesting!"

Maybe this girl would believe her. Misti looked down at her paper. "Everyone keeps telling me my locker is haunted."

"You got locker 31?"

Misti nodded.

Sarah shook her head. "You haven't heard the story?"

"What's the story?"

"I guess this girl was killed, like, 20 or 30 years ago. It happened around prom time. Her killer was never caught and anyone who's ever had that locker—her locker—has had issues."

"What issues?"

"Mental! One girl had a mental breakdown, like, ten years ago, screaming that there was a girl in the mirror who told her to hurt herself." Sarah shifted, wrinkling her eyes again. "They haven't let anyone else have it in a while." She tilted her head. "Seen anything yet?"

Misti forced a smile. "No, but if I do, you'll be the first to know."

The rest of her classes went smoothly. Sarah invited her to join her at lunch when she saw Misti sitting alone. Amber, the girl from the snack stand at the football game and who she had Art with sat at the table, looking over notes while eating at salad. She smiled at Misti when she sat down but was absorbed in her work. From her new vantage point, Misti could see a few tables over and spotted Alex, the boy from the football game and art class, watching her.

"Hey, Sarah, who is that guy? Alex?"

"Oh, yeah, Alex. Alex Turner. He's just a guy. Why?"

"He was talking to me at the football game on Friday. Was just curious."

"He's a nice guy." Sarah looked to Amber for comfomation. She just shrugged.

After lunch Misti returned to her locker, leaving her lunch companion who had a locker in a different hall. She stared hard at the lock, willing it to move, to show her she was not crazy. But it did not budge.

"Give yourself some credit; you were probably tired and upset because of the way things are going with Penny," she told herself. She grabbed her things for her afternoon classes.

In Art, Amber joined Misti at her empty table and produced the same notes from lunch.

"I have a huge exam in Anatomy tomorrow." She said when Misti finally asked what she was reading. "I have to be able to name all the muscles in the body." She sighed, placing her sketchpad out in front of her notes. Misti let her new companion study her notes and quietly doodled on her forest. Alex dropped his stuff on the table next to her, startling both girls.

"You said you'd help me!" he reminded her. Misti had said that. How unlike her. She didn't know if she really was enjoying some new things about her life. "Wow, that's really good!"

Misti covered her work, glancing at Amber who rolled her eyes at her notes.

"Thanks." She closed the cover. "How can I help you?"

Alex set his charcoal piece up on the counter. Misti offered the best advice she could and Alex listened intently, fetching more paper and doing as he was told. He was making a lot of little strokes and Misti encouraged him to do a solid line, going steady, pressing harder when he wanted a thicker, bolder line and pulling back when he didn't. Others were listening and soon trying what Misti suggested.

"Didn't Mr. Wilson tell you guys any of this?" Misti asked, looking around for their art teacher. She saw him sitting in the corner, one leg crossed over the other, his computer balanced on his knee.

"He just sits on his computer, playing poker online," Alex said.

"Oh." Misti felt disappointed. She was hoping to learn something.

"Yeah, this class is guaranteed A." Amber said. "That's why most of these people are here. Some of us actually want to try to learn. But we just have to teach ourselves." She had put her notes away and watched them intently.

"But now we have you!" Alex said. He sat up and grinned at her. "Better, right?"

It was better. Misti smiled back.

"I don't know much," she said to them, trying not to get their hopes up.

"Yeah, right," Amber rolled her eyes.

The bell rang and Misti packed up. She had spent the rest of the hour trying to help Amber. She was walking to her locker when Alex fell in pace beside her.

"Thanks for your help today. I really appreciate it. Art isn't really my thing, but it was this or Advanced Calculus. Guess which one my parents wanted me to take!"

"You're welcome."

"Maybe I can make it up to you?"

"Well, I'm not in Advanced Calculus but if I ever need help in Finance, I'll let you know."

"Cool! See you tomorrow!"

Misti thought she would come off as sarcastic, but Alex seemed oblivious to her tone. She shook her head and headed to her locker.

Nothing else odd happened, and she quickly grabbed her English things and creative writing notebook before heading out to the parking lot.

When she got there, Penny's car was gone. Maybe she got the area wrong. Misti walked slowly, looking around. The parking lot was not huge, and it did not take her long to realize that they had left her behind.

How freaking petty.

Sighing, she started down the sidewalk. She had gone about half a mile when there was a honk. Misti turned to see someone stopping next to her on a motorcycle.

"Hey!" The helmet came off and Alex's green eyes found hers. "You need a ride?"

"Uh," Misti did not know if riding on a motorcycle was something they allowed her to do. Her aunt and uncle were more concerned about little things than her mother. Then again, it was at least a three-mile walk to their house and she was tired. "Sure."

"Here, take my helmet," he said, shoving the black plastic into her hands. She pulled it over her hair and he started the bike again. She hesitated a moment before climbing on back, gently grabbing on. He gunned the bike, and she grabbed him tighter. She wondered if that had been his intention.

Seven

Added Tension

꒰ ꒱

They had only been moving for two minutes when Misti realized she had never told Alex where she lived. But he navigated with no issues, heading to her aunt and uncle's home. After the initial jolt, riding on the bike was more fun that she had expected. Things whizzed by quicker than they seemed to in cars.

Before long, they were slowing to a halt outside the house. Uncle Bill was just stepping out of his work van. His glare was easy to see from the driveway. He paused, arms crossed across his large chest, observing them through dark sunglasses. He said nothing, but Misti knew instinctively she was in trouble. It didn't seem fair. She was the one who got left behind at school by his daughter, who was perturbed because Misti had rolled her eyes at her tool of a love interest.

"Hey, Mr. McGrath!" Alex called after Misti had jumped off.

"Alex," Uncle Bill offered an acknowledgment, but his eyes settled on Misti.

Penny appeared in the doorway, carrying an apple, her eyes wide in wonder to see Alex standing there. Uncle Bill glanced at his daughter, offering her the same expression as he was Misti.

"Why did Misti need a ride home from him?" His tone held no anger, but Penny looked down.

"I had to stay late after school to work on a project with Alex. Something we are making in Art. I told Penny to leave and Alex offered me a ride." Misti heard herself say the words, heard herself cover for her cousin. Again. Penny looked up, her eyes meeting Misti's. Alex peered at Misti and then over at Penny, but revealed nothing to disprove her.

"Your parents let you ride that thing?" Uncle Bill's glare shifted to Alex.

Alex seemed unphased. He offered a shrug and a smirk. "They said if I got all As junior year I could get one."

Uncle Bill shook his head. "Thanks for bringing her home, but next time, she'll be in a car."

"Yes, sir." Alex gestured to Misti. "See you tomorrow." He tugged on the helmet and started the bike, speeding away.

Inside, Misti hung up her coat and her backpack.

"You're home early," Penny said. Misti wasn't sure if she was speaking to her or her father so she said nothing, crouching over and loosening her boots.

"I have to take Misti to an appointment." Misti looked up at him. "Sorry, we just found out. We have to leave in about ten minutes." Misti sighed and nodded. The state was not very considerate of people and their schedules. You had to do what they wanted, when they wanted. If you didn't, if she didn't, things could be bad not only for her but her uncle and aunt. She padded to the kitchen and listened to her uncle climb the stairs.

Penny came into the kitchen. When they heard the master door shut she said, "You didn't have to cover for me."

Misti shrugged. Her time of caring, the moment of choosing to protect her cousin, dissolved. Now she was furious that she had been left behind over a boy.

"How do you know Alex?"

Misti shrugged again.

Penny rolled her eyes and slapped her palm onto the counter. "You don't have to be like this!"

"Bold words from the person who just left me at school." Misti surprised herself at the evenness of her speech as she spread peanut butter onto toast.

Penny blushed. "That was Chloe's suggestion." As if she realized how foolish it was to blame someone else, she sighed. "I'm sorry. I shouldn't have. But you were rude to Tony."

"I was. I'll apologize to him next time I see him."

"That would mean a lot to me." Penny left the room, leaving Misti with a piece of bread covered in crunchy peanut butter. Misti knew that her relationship with Penny would never be what they had pretended it would be the first week here. Misti was the intruder and Penny was not used to sharing. And as she saw it, Tony was something that Misti wanted too and Misti doubted she could convince her otherwise.

The therapist was in a small building in the midst of downtown. On one side was a flower shop, on the other was a store sporting tie-dye blankets and smelling of incense. Her mother would have gone into that store and blown off the therapist immediately upon discovering it. The scent made her stomach crumble in on itself. Her mother had always smelled like that. Every place they ever lived had smelled like that.

The doctor's office smelled like Clorox wipes and defeat. There were two older chairs with a worn-out coffee table littered with magazines. They all turned out to be at least a year old. Uncle Bill plopped down in one chair and plucked up the car magazine, looking unamused. Misti fiddled with her bag. They had been there for about ten minutes when a younger man stepped out. He was holding a clipboard and wore Harry Potter glasses. His auburn hair was swept to one side. His brown eyes looked at her and she swore his glasses saw right through her.

"Misti, come on back!" he smiled. She knew it was meant to reassure her, but it only made her stomach pull back further. She glanced over at her uncle, and he gave her a stiff nod, a slight nudge to continue. She regretted that slice of bread.

Misti came into the office. It smelled much like the outside room only mixed with anguish.

"Sit wherever you like."

Was this a test? she wondered, looking at the big chair, reserved for him, the couch—she did not want to lie down like she saw so many movies portray—and a couple smaller chairs. She moved to the newer-looking chair and sat down.

"It's nice to meet you. I'm Dr. Smith."

"Hello," Misti said, setting her bag at her feet although she craved to hug it to her, like an insufficient security blanket. She needed something between them, something physical. He sat down in the big chair. First choice was correct.

"Have you done therapy before?"

Misti shook her head.

"Typically, I ask my patients what brings them here, but since you have come because the state is requiring you, I'll skip that part."

Misti pretended to smile. She thought he was trying to be funny. She searched around the office. It was ordinary, with a few licenses and diplomas hanging on the wall. There was one bookshelf with some nice leather-bound books and a few picture frames. The desk was clear except for a laptop computer and desk calendar.

61

"How are you feeling? There have been a number of changes for you over the past month."

"I'm okay."

The therapist looked down at his notes. "How are you enjoying living with your aunt, uncle, and cousin?"

"It's great. I have my own room. Aunt Mary took me shopping last weekend. That was something she didn't have to do. Uncle Bill is nice, but he works a bunch."

"And your cousin?"

"She's been wonderful. She helped me find all my classes, introduced me to people. I went with her to the football game last Friday and then to the drive-in afterwards. It was nice." Misti knew she needed to sell the state on her present situation. She was already inconveniencing everyone; she might as well let them see that her aunt and uncle had gone far beyond what she needed from them. She realized that whatever was going on with her and Penny was not therapist-worthy.

"I'm happy to hear things are going well." He looked at his notes again. He was trying to decide if he needed to ask about her mother, about that day, about that night. Misti didn't want him to. She had learned how to block out that day, at least during her waking hours. She dreamt about it enough to know that it was still there. Would talking really help her? She racked her brain for anything to change the subject, get him off-course.

"The kids at school told me I have a haunted locker." That was random. And it worked. He looked up from his notes, one eyebrow raised over his glasses. "I mean, I don't believe them, but everyone gets weird when I tell them that my locker number is 31."

"What do you mean 'weird'?" Good. He was off-track. Misti explained to him the attitude her classmates had when she informed them and she laughed about it. She did not tell him that this morning she thought she had seen the locker combination spinning. She was trying to convince him she was okay and didn't need to talk about her mother, not reinforce the fear of her mental instability.

"No one will tell me the story of what happened, though. So I doubt some girl died."

"Sounds like you're getting along pretty well in your school."

Misti shrugged. She thought about telling him it wasn't the first time she had to enroll into a new school and learn to navigate the norms. She was only so successful this time because of Penny. Maybe she should talk about that.

"My cousin really helped me out the first few days. It was a lot easier going to this school. I wasn't alone."

The session concluded on a good note. Uncle Bill was still in the waiting room, reading a different car magazine. They drove home in silence, listening to the radio. They were sitting at one of the three stoplights in the small town when Misti saw a 'help wanted' sign in the coffee shop window.

"Uncle Bill?" she said. "Would it be all right if I tried to get a job?"

He looked over at her, surprised.

"I'm used to having one," she told him.

He smiled. "I suggested to Penny once that she get a job. You would have thought I'd asked her to cut off her leg."

Misti knew that Penny would struggle with a job; she did too much at school. But Misti was bored in her classes and she knew that now she was caught up, her senior year would be smooth. Plus, she would like to save up for after she finished. She would have to be ready to move.

"Where would you apply?" Uncle Bill asked as they turned down their street.

"Anywhere that was hiring. I've worked at a few places before. I enjoyed waitressing and stocking shelves." She pointed out the window.

"Blackwood Coffee is hiring."

Uncle Bill did not know about any of this. He seemed impressed. And that made Misti happy. "I'll talk to your aunt and see what she thinks. But I think it's a fine idea."

Aunt Mary was in the kitchen when they came in. She hurried into the hall as they took off their coats and set their shoes in their assigned places. Misti wondered if her uncle would do any of this if not for her aunt.

"How was it?" Aunt Mary was clutching a towel, as if choking the life out of it. Her eyes looked half crazed. She must have been home for a while, working herself up into this frenzied state.

"It was fine." Uncle Bill kissed his wife hello and moved past her. Misti smiled at her aunt and nodded in agreement.

"Are you sure?" Aunt Mary began to deflate.

"Sure!" Misti said, going out of the entryway to the kitchen. Her uncle was at the fridge, inspecting it carefully. He removed a beer gingerly, cracking it open, and looked at his wife.

"It wasn't like they would hook wires to her and poke and prod her. They just want to talk to her."

"Did you speak to him after?"

"No."

"When is the next appointment?"

Uncle Bill set down his beer and retrieved his wallet. He pulled out a card and handed it to his wife.

"I can take off early on Tuesdays to get her there," he said, before going to the couch and plopping down. Aunt Mary looked at the card before handing it to Misti. She would have to go to the office twice a month on Tuesdays at 4.

"I could probably just walk," Misti said, wanting to be less of a burden. "It's only a few blocks from school."

"And I can pick you up," Aunt Mary nodded, as if they had decided it.

Uncle Bill looked at Misti when she sat down, impressed again. "We still have to talk about your motorcycle ride today." Okay, maybe not impressed.

"Motorcycle ride?" Aunt Mary was inflating again.

"Alex Turner gave Misti a ride home from school today. On the back of his motorcycle."

"Misti! You know that we do not..." Aunt Mary stopped and looked at her husband, who was now looking amused.

"Misti," Aunt Mary sat down. Misti realized that her aunt and uncle had never given her any expectations and she was about to get them. She wondered what this would be like, being given rules. She used to just make rules for herself. Common sense stuff really, like never go to a boy's house alone, never date guys out of high school, don't do drugs, and don't drink. The last two she learned early. She had seen what they did to you and didn't need to experience it herself.

"We don't mind you having friends and getting rides. But we do not want you riding on a motorcycle. They're dangerous. We just want you to be safe."

"Okay," Misti said.

Aunt Mary let out the breath she was holding and looked at her husband, eyebrows up in shock.

Uncle Bill laughed. "I didn't know, but I'll make sure it doesn't happen again."

"Thank you," Aunt Mary looked at her. "Can I ask why you got a ride from him?"

"Group project. We had to stay late to work on it. I didn't want Penny to wait around and he offered me a ride. I didn't know it was on a motorcycle." She had to keep the story straight for Penny.

"Well, while we have you here, I guess we better discuss our other expectations for you."

They were basic: Curfew was midnight on weekends and nine on weekdays. Homework would be completed and there would be no failing of classes. Chores needed to be done daily and she would be in charge of sweeping and mopping on weekends now. She would also be in charge of cleaning the shared bathroom every other week. If she wanted to borrow one of their cars, she just needed to let them know in advance.

"I don't know how to drive," Misti shrugged. "So that won't be a problem."

Aunt Mary teared up and looked to her husband, who leaned forward and squeezed his wife's hand.

"Did I say something wrong?"

"No! I just…" Aunt Mary grabbed a tissue. "Every teenager should learn to drive!"

Misti shrugged. "We never had a car for long and we lived in the city. There was always a way to get to where you needed to go."

Aunt Mary looked upset again. Lesson learned: Do not talk about the past.

Penny came into the room then. "Mom, are you okay?"

"Yes, dear, just talking to Misti about some things." Aunt Mary stood and clapped her hands together, taking a long, loud breath. "Who's hungry?"

They ate a quiet meal, Penny talking about yearbook stuff and Misti trying to figure out how best to avoid upsetting her aunt again. Dinner was wrapping up when Uncle Bill said, "Misti asked me if she could apply for some jobs. I think it would be a good idea. But I told her we needed to talk to you first."

Aunt Mary looked taken aback and Penny glared at Misti.

"I don't see why she shouldn't be able to. Do you think you can handle school and work?"

"Sure," Misti said. She didn't add that she had done it before and didn't tell her about her preferred jobs. Uncle Bill knew that she had worked before. Plus, she didn't want her aunt knowing that she had been working odd jobs since she was fourteen. The past summer, she had worked two jobs to keep her and her mother's heads above water. And to stay out of the house as much as possible. Her mother had been with a weird man at the time and Misti never liked him. She had stayed with a coworker most of that summer. She was a few years older than Misti and never asked her why she didn't want to go home. This last month had been the longest she had gone without a job.

"Okay."

Misti had not returned to her room since leaving it that morning. She found just stepping across the threshold soothed her. She closed the door and went to bed, plopping down on it. She closed her eyes and thought about the day. So much had happened. She pushed aside her feelings of being forced to see the therapist, the tears in her aunt's eyes, the anger in Penny's, and instead focused on the locker. She saw in her mind the combination of black and silver with tiny numbers, slowly rotating. She was tired this morning. She never slept well on Sunday nights. She was a little annoyed with Penny. She was just imagining things, like she was right in that moment. She could make her mind spin the numbers in one direction and then the other, faster and slower.

Her locked was not haunted.

Dear J,

Today was a weird day. First, Penny has decided I am the enemy because she likes a dumb guy who thinks he is so hot. Really, he is just one of those guys that is so insecure he had to point out all that is wrong with others to keep the focus off himself. Also, Penny really could do better. I don't understand why she is so obsessed with him.

The therapist wasn't as bad as I was expecting. I guess I had hoped that we would not even have to go. I mean, the state had dropped the ball so many times, why not this time too?

Uncle Bill is warming up to me. He seems happy that I want to get a job. But Penny is upset again. Probably because they want her to have a job and she won't get one. She does take a lot of hard classes. Maybe she shouldn't. Because she clearly makes bad choices. Like leaving me today.

I hope Alex and I can be friends. And I hope he knows that it can never be more. Because I am too damaged for that.

The locker combination was not spinning.

Eight

The Dream

~⚬ᘓᕲᕆᕲᘐ⚬~

Misti had a nightmare for the first time since arriving at the McGrath home. She recognized the signs of the nightmare instantly . The hues were all off and the proportions were erroneous. The fear tickled the back of her neck, teasing her as she moved. She was back on the old route, walking home from work. It was late and Misti felt apprehension in her chest as she walked, gripping the knife she carried in her pocket. No one ever approached her, but she saw enough questionable characters on her walk to justify having the knife. They had no faces now—not that Misti ever noticed their faces in real life. She did her best to sink into the background as she went. She didn't wish to draw attention to herself. She didn't want to use the knife. She walked faster, eyes downcast. They never grabbed for her, just stayed off to the side. She reached the steps that led up to the apartment building she and her mother were staying in. The school had allowed Misti to work for most of the day. She would wake at 6 and be at school by 8. By noon, she was working at the restaurant, helping with the lunch rush and again the dinner rush. The tips were so good she hid her money. For an escape? She didn't know. She could never abandon her mother. Could she? She invariably had these thoughts as she mounted the steps. Every night. Dread started at the tip of her spine and slowly tumbled down her back, a little splash at a time. An old rap song was coming from the apartment on the first floor.

Misti willed herself to wake up. She didn't need to see this again.

Her dream body would not listen. She began the climb to the third floor. The hallway light was out, so she used the outline of the lights from other doors to find number 14.

Wake up, wake up, wake up!

The door opened and Misti was screaming.

"Misti!"

Misti finally tore her eyes open. Hands were holding her arms, and she was in a comfortable bed, in a quiet room. Standing over her was her uncle. He did not look annoyed, or amused, or impressed. She did not know how he looked. She was breathing hard, her sheets were in a tangle around her, hair matted against her forehead.

"It's okay," he said, releasing her arms. Misti slowly pushed herself up, taking in the space, trying to calm her heart. In the doorway stood Penny. She looked at her, scared.

"I'm sorry," Misti said.

"You were having a nightmare." Uncle Bill gently smoothed her hair. Misti felt tears well inside of her but forced them down. She nodded.

"Penny, go get her a glass of water."

Misti looked down her her hands. They were trembling.

"Do you want to talk about it?"

Misti shook her head. She didn't need to relive that moment, ever again.

Uncle Bill sat with her, his large hand close to but not touching her. "Mary takes sleeping pills from time to time," he said. "Lucky for us, tonight was one of those nights."

Penny appeared with the glass. Misti took it, avoiding eye contact with her cousin.

"I don't think this is something Mary needs to know about right now." Uncle Bill looked at his daughter, who looked surprised before nodding.

"Do you need me to stay?" Uncle Bill asked. Misti shook her head. Her heart was still thumping hard in her chest and her throat had a knot in it. She needed them to leave. Uncle Bill gently stood, putting his arm around Penny. "Try to go back to sleep. I know this doesn't help, but it was just a dream."

But it wasn't. It had been reality only a few weeks ago. The people had faces, but that song had been the same. The lights in the hall had been out, and that is what she had opened her door to.

But Misti couldn't tell them that. Because she was already causing too much of an issue. Her aunt had to take a sleeping pill tonight. Because of her. Her aunt was stressed because of her. She didn't need to make it worse.

Misti cried for the first time in three weeks after they shut the door. She turned her face to the pillow and cried as quietly as she could.

It was more than a dream; it was a memory. It had happened.

Misti did not allow herself to sleep the rest of the night. She stayed in bed, watching the hours tick by. At 6am, she prepared for school and came downstairs to find her uncle out of bed, drinking coffee and watching the news. Her aunt was not in the kitchen yet. Penny was in the shower.

"Sorry," Misti said hoarsely.

Uncle Bill looked at her, confused.

"About last night."

"You can't control your dreams," Uncle Bill sighed. "I'm sure it stirred

71

things up yesterday, having to go see that therapist."

Misti nodded. She was okay with blaming that guy.

"You know, you can always talk to me about anything you want," Uncle Bill told her.

Misti nodded. She felt a little warmth return to her chest. It was nice knowing that she didn't have to keep this secret if she didn't want to. She knew her uncle would listen and, if he got upset, he could hide it. For her.

School was foggy that day. Misti was drained and Penny was not speaking to her. Misti wasn't certain if it was because of the dream or because of Tony. The combination on the locker did not twirl, so Misti dismissed it.

By the time lunch rolled around, Misti just needed to take a nap somewhere. She pulled her lunch from her locker and turned towards the lunchroom. She was so out of it she was alarmed to hear her name.

Misti looked to her left and her stomach fell. It was Tony. He was sporting a sweater and jeans, his hair brushed forward with too much gel. He had morphed from wanna be jock guy to sleezy salesman.

"So, you have the haunted locker? Anything cool happen yet?"

Misti frowned and shook her head. Like she would tell him.

"Penny said you wanted to speak to me?" he smirked.

Misti's skin crawled. Hopefully she could keep her personal feelings off her face. That took a lot of effort even when she was rested. "Oh, yeah. I just needed to apologize about the other night. I shouldn't have said those things."

Tony's grin grew, and he took a step closer to her. "I know. You were just trying to make an impression." Misti took a step backward.

"You need to know that I knew that."

Misti felt an eye roll coming and turned, heading towards the lunchroom. Tony fell into step beside her. She made sure to keep a safe distance between them.

"Penny really likes you," Misti heard herself say.

"I know," he shrugged. Misti got the impression that he didn't really like her back.. "I'll let her know you apologized. See you." He winked at her and strode towards the jock table. Misti started at the table with the Sarah and saw Penny watching her. She offered her a nod and Penny smiled at her. Misti felt bad for her cousin for only a moment. She picked such a loser.

By Art, Misti was done. She sat at the table sketching the street from her dream last night, drawing outlines of the faceless bodies.

"That is so cool," Amber said, peering over her shoulder. "Where did you get that idea?"

"Just sort of came to me," Misti said. "Probably saw it on TV or something."

Misti looked at Amber's drawing. It wasn't the best she had seen, but it had potential. It was a landscape, but the trees were scratchy and uninviting.

"Yours is good too," Misti said.

Amber shrugged. "I prefer abstract, but I never finished my landscape assignment from a month ago. Mr. Wilson only cares about grades when they are due. And I only care about this class because I have a scholarship waiting for me. I can't screw up one class now."

Misti listened to Amber ramble on about her college choices and how hard it had been for her to decide. And now that she had decided, waiting to hear if that college even wanted her was the worst part of it all. Misti nodded and stared, her fatigued state making it futile to accomplish any tasks now. She had twenty minutes left in class and since there were three girls who she had yet to see put their phones down and complete any work, she guessed she was safe to gawk at the picture in her hands.

"You look tired." Alex plopped next to her, dropping his bag to the floor. Misti looked over at him. Had he just come into class? Did Mr. Wilson even notice? Looking at the art teacher, he looked as if his online betting was not working out today.

"You never tell a woman she looks tired, Alex!" Amber said. "It's disparaging."

"Why? She looks sleepy and I'm not trying to be rude, I'm checking on her."

"It's harsh. You could just ask how she was managing."

"Okay. Hey, Misti, how are you managing? You don't look exhausted at all."

Amber rolled her eyes and turned her attention back to her landscape.

"It's okay, Alex, I am tired. I didn't sleep last night." She wasn't mad at him for noticing. In fact, he was the only one who had acknowledged it today. At lunch Sarah and Amber had been having a profound debate about feminism and Amber had just chatted about herself for the class, outside liking Misti's picture.

"Everything okay?"

"Yes, just couldn't sleep."

"Did I get you in trouble?"

Misti smiled and shook her head.

"No, my uncle and aunt realized that they had actually never told me their rules when I moved in. But, just so you know, I'm not allowed on the bike anymore."

"Fair enough. My dad hates it anyway. And it really is too cold to drive it right now. I think I should just sell it."

Misti was bewildered. He would stop driving his bike because she couldn't ride it or because he didn't want to anymore? She was reading too much into the situation.

Alex pulled out his sketchbook and Misti saw that he had spent some time since the last class practicing the things she had told him. Maybe he wanted to learn. He let her sit while he practiced, never asking her for advice but letting her watch him. Misti enjoyed his silent company.

The twenty minutes took an hour to pass. She gathered her things and zombie-walked to her locker. It took her a moment to understand that Alex was wandering with her.

"Do you need another ride today?"

Misti honestly didn't know. She had apologized to Tony and hoped that would mend the fences with Penny. And since calling her out on her behavior yesterday, she would have a lift home. But she had stirred the pot last night when she asked if she could get a job.

"I don't know. I have to find my cousin."

"Well, I'll hang out until you do, just in case. I don't enjoy leaving right away, anyway. There's too much traffic."

Misti wanted to laugh at him. There was no such thing as traffic in this town.

They arrived at her locker and Misti opened it. Everything she needed for that night sat neatly in a pile on the top shelf, while her unneeded supplies were assembled at the bottom of the locker, in order of her classes, for tomorrow.

"What's wrong?"

"Nothing," Misti said. She must have done that right after lunch. She grabbed the few things she needed and slammed the locker shut. "I hear my locker is haunted."

Alex rolled his eyes. "That's just a myth. Ghosts aren't real."

"Maybe," Misti said as they left the building together. She was happy to find Penny waiting for her on the bottom steps. She was talking to Tony. "Guess I do have a ride."

"Cool, well, if you ever need one, let me know." Alex half waved to her and headed in the opposite direction, hands in his pockets. Misti watched him go, feeling a little sad she didn't get to ride home with the strange boy today.

"Ready to go?" Penny called up to her. Tony was watching Alex walk away. For once, he didn't look confident.

"You and Alex seem to get along pretty well," Penny commented. Her voice was casual, but Misti could tell she was fishing. Misti just shrugged. She didn't have the energy for whatever Penny wanted from her. But maybe since she had walked outside with a different boy, Penny would forgive her for Tony. "Tony told me you apologized. That means a lot to me. Thank you."

"You're welcome," Misti grumbled. She had a headache. She needed to lie down for a few minutes.

"He wants us to come to the game on Saturday. It's a big one." Misti nodded, not hearing her. "I might go to the party after." Misti was listening now. She had only been at the school for a few weeks and she knew what the party was. "What? Chloe thinks it would be fun."

Misti had witnessed enough 'fun times' in her life and searched for the words, for the perfect way, to explain to Penny about 'fun times'. But her cloudy head prevented her. "I don't think they sound fun."

"Well, I'm sure for a girl from the city it probably wouldn't. But we have to make our own fun here." Penny was gripping the steering wheel. She was mad again. Misti kept her mouth closed the rest of the way home.

They were the first ones back. After taking off her shoes, Misti climbed the stairs to her room and collapsed into bed. She set the alarm clock for 5pm and fell asleep. She just wanted enough sleep to get her through the evening.

She woke thirty minutes later with a pounding headache. She lay there in the evening light before convincing herself to get up and go find medicine. Her aunt was downstairs, just arrived home, still wearing her work clothes and looking through the mail.

"Misti, what's wrong?" Aunt Mary set down the mail and was to

Misti in three steps, a warm hand coming to her forehead.

"I have a headache," Misti said.

"Sit down, sweetie, I'll get you some water and pills."

Misti sat at the bar and her aunt hurried to the cabinet, got a glass, filled it with water and fetched a bottle of pills from above the oven. Misti accepted the glass and pills and swallowed them quickly.

"Tough day?"

Misti thought for a moment. She wondered if she should tell her aunt about not sleeping well, about the nightmare, about not wanting to go back to that therapist because he would make her think about it again and if that happened, the nightmare would only get worse. But then she remembered the tears in her aunt's eyes when Misti said she had never learned to drive. And if she couldn't handle that...

"Just a lot of dumb people today." That was something Penny would say. Aunt Mary smiled.

"I wish I could tell you that that goes away." Aunt Mary went to the fridge and talked her way through what they would have for dinner. By the time the decision was made to have chicken thighs and dirty rice, the headache was easing up.

Misti went to bed right after she finished her chores. She did her reading and what she had to do for the rest of the project with Sarah. She finished her three math problems. Then she laid down. By the time she had finished, her headache was back. She forced herself to shower before crawling into bed.

She was just about to doze off when her phone buzzed.

I didn't know how to say this at school but I think you should know. Penny told me about your mom. I'm really sorry about all that. I get your distance now.

Betrayal. Icy hot betrayal hit her hard in her chest. For the second time that day, she cried.

Nine

The Face

∽⟨ֆⓄֆⓄ⟩∽

"Alex and Tony used to be best friends," Penny said. They were on their way to school. The comment came out of the blue. Misti had not told Penny about Alex's text last night. She rotated between furious and betrayed.

"Used to be?" Misti reminded herself that she was the intruder here and needed to play the game. But so far, Penny had not been playing fair. And she was ready to snap.

"All the way through middle school. But when they got to high school, something happened and they stopped talking."

Misti supposed that happened. People grow and change. Most people at least.

When they arrived at the school, Chloe was waiting for Penny in their usual meeting spot.

Penny and Misti said goodbye to each other and Misti bolted up the stairs to her locker. Penny had been running a little late that morning so Misti was in a rush. She was surprised to find Alex waiting for her, two coffees from Blackwood Coffee in hand.

"Good morning!" he said, holding out the drink to her. "It's a cappuccino. Just in case you didn't sleep well again." Cute and thoughtful. And not scared about her mom?

Misti thanked him while unlocking her locker. Nothing was out of place this time. It was exactly how she had left it. She set the coffee on the shelf and put her lunch pail away along with her supplies for her afternoon classes. Why was he was being so nice? Pity?

"How was the rest of your evening?"

"Fine. Went to bed early." She shrugged on her pack again and took down her coffee. She glanced in the mirror. Why was she checking to make sure she looked okay? She smoothed out a wave that was starting to frizz and wiped away a fleck of black from her mascara. She saw movement and looked to see who was passing them. A girl, wearing a flowing dress and bathed in green light, seemed to be floating towards her. Every hair on Misti's arms stood on edge. The girl's eyes were black and her skin a sickly blue. Her clothes floated around her, as if she was in a pool of water. She began to raise her hand, reaching for something. Misti glanced over her shoulder.

Alex made a puzzled face and also glanced over his shoulder. "What's wrong?"

Misti looked back at the mirror. A face other than her own was staring back. The face belonged to the girl who had just been behind her. She opened her mouth, maybe to scream, maybe to say something. Misti gasped, slamming the locker shut, jerking her coffee, spilling it all over her hand and the floor.

"Jesus! Are you okay?" Alex grabbed her arm, supporting her. "What's wrong?"

Misti looked over her shoulder, but only a few people passed. They all glanced at her and the spilled coffee, offering sympathic smiles as they continued on their way.

"Misti?" She was shaking and Alex sounded concerned.

"Sorry, I thought..." she stopped herself and remembered the stories of the others who had the locker before her, claiming they saw someone; a girl. She also remembered Sarah's word choice describing them. She called them mental. Misti did not want to be seen as mental or anything close to that. "Nothing, I'm fine."

Alex didn't look convinced but he hurried to the boys' bathroom and returned with a handful of paper towels, helping her to clean up her mess and herself. Misti kept glancing at the locker. What the hell was that?

They walked to her first class. Misti was distracted and Alex did his best to pretend she hadn't just done something weird. Sarah passed them, saying hey.

Ms. Williams had changed the quote on her sign: "Truth is not what it seems, but what it is."

She probably meant it to tie into *To Kill a Mockingbird*, but after all the odd things that had happened, Misti wondered if the rumor about her locker was true. She needed to know the story.

"Are you sure you're okay?" Alex stopped by the door to her class.

"Yeah. I'll explain later." Before she knew it, Alex was hugging her and moving away. It was a hug and run. Misti could still feel the warmth of his brief embrace as she sat down. Ms. Williams was not there. It was an old sub who announced they were to start on a project and any messing around would result in a referral to the office.

"I saw that hug!" Sarah said in a voice that almost sung the last word.

"Yeah, that was weird," Misti took a sip of her coffee and wondered how Alex knew she would love caramel.

Sarah didn't say much more.

The girls got to work on their project. They did their best to look busy to avoid the wrath of the sub who was pacing in the front, holding a newspaper behind her back. She wore an outfit from the 1970s: green slacks and a matching floral top. And orthopedic shoes.

"Do you remember when you told me those things about my locker?"
Sarah nodded, writing out the title for their project carefully.

"Do you know who it is that's supposed to be haunting it?"
Sarah turned her eyes to her.

"Has something happened?" She looked hopeful. Misti wondered
if Sarah would think she was crazy or if she would believe her. She
looked like she would believe her. But what if she thought she was
crazy?

"No; I'm just curious."

Sarah sighed and said she didn't know more than what she had told
her before. "You tell me if something happens." Sarah spent the rest of
the class telling Misti all the paranormal and spooky things she had
ever experienced. Most were stories of creepy feelings and thinking
she heard something. Nothing like what Misti had experienced that
morning. Maybe Misti was going crazy. She needed to find out the
story.

Amber might know.

"I don't know for sure. I think the girl who owned it was murdered?
Or died somehow? Like back in the 90s," Amber told her during lunch
that day. She had notes for her economics class out today. She didn't
look too concerned with Misti's question.

"Why are you so curious? I thought you said nothing was happening?" Sarah's mouth was full.

"Nothing has. I'm just wondering why everyone is so skittish. Also,
there's always a little bit of truth, or history, in those stories. I could
use it for creative writing class." Misti impressed herself with that lie.
It came out so quickly.

Sarah rolled her eyes and looked over the tables to where Alex sat
with some other boys.

"Why don't you ask Alex?"

Misti shrugged, taking a bite of her sandwich. Amber perked up, interested in this topic.

"Are you and Alex a thing?"

"No."

"He walked her to first hour and brought her a coffee," Sarah dished.

Amber grinned at Misti. "He's a catch! He doesn't date just anyone. Last I heard, he was dating a girl who was on her way to being a model."

Misti thought that couldn't be true and was also a little flattered. And insulted. Then she remembered the beautiful girl at the football game. She could have been a model of some sort she supposed. But aren't all models tall?

"I'm not at a point in my life where I want a relationship," Misti said. The two girls looked at her unconvinced. "I mean, I just moved here and I'm still dealing with what happened…" Misti stopped herself short. She was not about to share with these two. She liked them too much and that was way too much information. But both girls moved in curiously.

"What happened?"

Misti took another bite of her sandwich, her appetite suddenly gone.

"Just some stuff with my mom." She knew her voice was low. "I don't really want to talk about it."

Both girls respected her wishes and changed the subject to the rumors of how crazy "the party" was going to get that weekend. Misti listened half-heartedly.

"I don't know the story, just rumors." Alex sat on the table, his arms crossed, looking down at her. He was not working on art today, apparently. Misti sat with her sketchbook in front of her, the drawing from her nightmare half finished. She wasn't sure she wanted to finish it. "We could probably do some research, if you really wanted to know."

"That's okay. I'll just come up with a new story idea. Or make one up."

"I can't even!" Amber threw down her pencil in frustration. Misti and Alex looked over at her. She was attempting a self-portrait and it actually didn't look half bad. But Amber was a perfectionist.

"Looks like a Picasso," Alex said, tilting his head and squinting before grinning.

"Har-har. At least I'm working!" Amber stared at her paper.

"It looks great. Maybe try shading in more here," Misti suggested, pointing to a couple points. Amber eagerly took the advice.

Alex sat down and pulled out his sketchpad. "How about I do you Misti, and you do me?"

"That's what she said," Amber whispered, and Alex and Misti blushed.

"Sure," Misti said. She would much prefer to sketch Alex than herself. She decided to sketch Alex as he was sketching—his forehead a little wrinkled in concentration, his eyes focused on the pad in his hands. A strand of his dark hair was falling slightly out of place, and his lips were slightly parted. She was halfway done when the bell rang.

"Can I see?" he asked.

"When it's done."

"Same for you!" He shoved his notebook into his pack and they headed out of the class.

"See you guys tomorrow!" Amber headed down the hall, going to debate practice.

"Can I give you a ride?" Alex asked. Misti wanted to say no, but she didn't know of a way to say it nicely, so she simply nodded.

At her locker, Misti found all the things she needed to take home neatly stacked and waiting for her again. This time, she knew she had not done that. It made her skin crawl.

"So organized," Alex said, watching her take all those things and place them carefully in her pack. She considered telling him what she thought was going on. Instead, she closed the door, knowing that if she looked in the mirror she would see another face staring back at her.

"Thanks," she said quietly, to the locker, but knowing Alex would think it was to him.

Misti texted Penny and told her Alex would be giving her a ride. Penny sent back a thumbs up symbol and a kissy face.

Alex took a long route to her house, Misti thinking about the locker and Alex singing along with the radio. He joked that having a car and a motorcycle was one perk of having a rich father.

They stopped outside of her aunt and uncle's house. She knew she needed to tell him. "Alex, I need to be honest with you."

"You have a boyfriend back in the city." He said it so quickly, she wondered how long he had been thinking about that. He had turned his eyes to the radio, fiddling with the buttons.

"What? No!" He turned his face back to her and she saw it lighten with hope. "I know that Penny told you about my mom. Or something about my mom. It's just that…" She paused, wondering how she could tell him this without being a total bitch. "I just went through something; something pretty big. I'm not ready to talk about it. And I also don't think I'm ready to be more than friends with anyone. Because, right now, I'm still dealing with what happened. And I wouldn't be able to fully invest myself in a relationship." She fiddled with the seat belt. "I mean, with everything that happened with my mom…" she trailed off, not wanting to add in more.

Alex stared at her, his face not changing. "I understand."

There was no hurt in his voice. She had not destroyed him. Instead, he had confused her.

"I hope we can still be friends."

He smiled, reached across the center console and took her hand.

"I would like that. And I'm not pressuring you. I'll be here if you ever decide you want something more, though."

"You'll find another girl before that happens." Misti was thinking about the beautiful Emily and her large round eyes.

"Bet."

Penny was sitting on the stairs bouncing with excitement when she came in.

"I tried spying on you through the window but I realized that was, like, beyond creepy so I came here instead. Did you kiss? Are you guys dating or just talking?"

"We're just friends." Misti hung up her jacket and backpack.

"Yeah, right!"

"You pretty much made sure of that when you told him about my mom and why I'm here. Wasn't that your plan? Or was that another one of Chloe's ideas?"

Penny froze, mouth ajar. "I..."

"You what? Thought that it was okay to tell my friends my business? Do you think it's easy for me being here? I have spent the last few weeks tiptoeing around you, doing everything you want of me and I'm done! I can't do it anymore! Who else did you tell? Amber and Sarah, the only other people at school who don't look at me like I'm a crazy outsider?" Misti stopped herself, holding back the lump of tears in her throat.

"Misti," Penny was quiet.

Misti pulled down her bag and went up to her room, slamming the door shut. She had done everything that girl had asked and this was how she repaid her?

Misti had math homework to do. She dumped out her things from her backpack. A tiny leather-bound notebook tumbled to the ground. She dropped her bag and had to get on the floor. She found the notebook under her bed. She did not recognize it. It was small, but the leather was soft and there was a short length of ribbon sticking out of the pages. There was no writing on the cover. She sat back on her knees and opened the book. In the front cover in nice cursive it read: "Property of Lily Banks."

Misti smelled dust and an old perfume coming up from the pages. No one had opened the book in a while.

December 25th 1999

I am so excited to have this new, adult journal. I told Mother that I wanted one to replace that old Lisa Frank one! I can't believe I even used to like that stuff! And the lock on it was a joke. I know that Matthew broke into it the first week I had it and told all the boys in my class that had made my cute list. Ugh!

   I'm planning on taking this journal with me so I can write my thoughts when I need to.

The journal went on to talk about what else she had gotten, what her brother had gotten, and what a beautiful necklace her father had gotten her mother.

Where did this come from? And who was Lily Banks?

Ten

Introductions

 ⚬ᘓᘓ⚬

Misti sat on the floor for the next hour, reading page after page. For the first several entries, Lily wrote about what seemed to be a typical and even boring life. She complained about her classes, her brother, and her mother. She sometimes discussed her father. She talked about her best friend Shannon and how excited they were for summer and sitting at the pool. She talked about her on-again, off-again boyfriend, Brian. Brian, it appeared, was interested in more than just kissing and holding hands, but Lily wasn't ready for that. He would often dump her and her world would be over for a few weeks, but somehow they always got back together. The entries were sporadic, sometimes an entry not coming for months after the last one. The biggest gap happened between May and October 1999. And that is where things got very interesting.

October 9, 1999

I can't believe I'm doing this. Tonight, I'm sneaking out after bed to meet him. I'm not going to write his name, just in case Matthew gets a hold of this. I know this is wrong but I don't care. He is so handsome, even more than George Clooney or Brad Pitt! And the fact that he is older doesn't bother me. It just means he is more mature and able to take care of me. I just still can't believe that he noticed me of all people.

This was not Brian she was talking about. She knew Brian was in the same grade as Lily and Shannon. Lily had spent an entire page complaining about how immature he was, giving examples of laughing at stupid words and making dumb jokes with his friends at the drive-in. Although Misti assumed they were still together, she couldn't be sure. It wouldn't be hard to imagine that they had broken up.

October 10, 1999

I did it and he was there, in his car, waiting for me. I tried to be calm when I got in but my heart was beating so fast! He drove us to his house, and we sat up most of the night just talking! It was so nice to just have a conversation with someone!

He brought me back home just before 4 and we kissed! He didn't even try to undo my bra like Brian does!

Gosh, I am so tired but I could hardly sleep! This has been the most exciting thing I have like ever done! Shannon doesn't even know about it! We have to keep it a secret. He could get in a lot of trouble. Society has rules and they just don't get that two people sometimes just have a connection. And that doesn't make it wrong on the spiritual level. Just on the level of their rules.

It intrigued Misti. The last part was not anything Lily would have said before. Most of her writing had been very surface level. That was a little much. She must have written what the mysterious suitor had said to convince her to meet him.

Who was he?

Misti looked at the clock. It was close to 6. She had math homework to do. And the nightly family dinner. She wanted to keep reading, see if she could find out who the mysterious man was, but she put the diary back in her bag and got up to go to dinner. After dinner, Misti struggled with her math homework. By the time she finished, she was too brain dead the finish the diary.

Misti dreamed of a beautiful girl, wearing a typical 1990s outfit, curly, puffy hair and a jean jacket with a jean skirt, walking down the halls of her school. She was laughing with another girl. The second girl was not as pretty as the first, with short brown hair and a piggish nose. Misti recognized the hall. It was her school. The floors were shining from wax and the lockers were a faded yellow. Misti watched this scene play out before her like an old home film with no sound. A boy approached the girls and the pretty jean jacket girl talked to him for a while, but they were not happy with each other. The boy threw up a hand in frustration, as the girls pushed past him. The girls moved away and stopped at a locker. The camera zoomed in on the locker number: 31. The face of the jean jacket girl filled the frame, and she was not smiling anymore. She was looking straight at Misti. Her face changed color, going to a green-gray, her eyes turning black and her hair losing its shape and becoming stringy. The face from the mirror. She was opening her mouth again.

Misti bolted awake.

It was 4am, and the house was quiet. Misti breathed a sigh of relief. This dream, at least, had not woken the family. Misti wanted to grab the journal and keep reading. But she forced herself to lie back down. She knew that she wouldn't be able to go back to sleep, but she could make herself think about this rationally.

This journal had appeared out of nowhere, just one of a series of off things that had occurred at her locker. But Misti did not believe in ghosts. And how could a ghost give her an old diary? Maybe it had been stuck in there and had just fallen among her things? The diary was 20 years old. Who knew when it was put in the locker.

But the face of the girl that Misti saw in the locker the day before could just be her mind combining the two thoughts. In reality, she would never be able to tell anyone this, because they would think she was crazy.

Just like her mother.

Misti squeezed her eyes shut.

She was not crazy. She knew that. But these things happening were not helping her.

She really wished she could talk to someone. She had just screamed at Penny about her sharing her secrets. Besides that, she could tell Penny had been uncomfortable just standing next to the locker. Sarah would be very interested but after all her stories of ghostly encounters, this was beyond her. How would she even start that conversation?

"Remember how I told you nothing weird was happening. Well, I lied."

Not a great way to start a friendship.

There was her therapist—who was working for the state and probably reporting back to them on her mental stability. The last thing she needed was give to them any fuel for the fire they were building. Her mother had done enough on her own; Misti didn't need to add to it. Besides, she had no way of backing any of this up. The diary could be one she had found in a thrift shop or even wrote herself.

Alex. Of all people, she could probably tell Alex. She knew that he would listen, just like he did today, and probably not judge her. He might laugh. He would want to see the diary. But he wouldn't judge her. She knew that in her soul.

But she wouldn't tell him, because she just wanted to be friends.

Misti dozed off around 5:30 and woke sharply at 6:15. Her head was groggy. She cursed herself, knowing she probably should have stayed awake.

She dressed and grabbed her things, checking for her math homework and the diary before heading down the stairs. Her uncle was awake, looking like she felt. He nodded to acknowledge her existence, but she had learned that her uncle was a zombie until he had a third cup of coffee in his system. Misti mulled over her cereal, still thinking about Lily Banks.

Misti had mixed feelings when she arrived at her locker and Alex was not there. She could face the locker and whatever surprises it held alone, but she also knew that, despite his brave face yesterday, she might have lost a friend.

She opened the locker and was not surprised to find what she needed waiting for her.

"Hey, Lily," she said under her breath. "Thanks!" She transferred a few things. "I, um, started your diary. I hope that's okay. I mean, I hope that's what you wanted me to do." There was no response. Misti hadn't expected one.

"Who are you talking to?"

Misti spun around, knocking her hand hard into her locker door.

Alex stood there, coffee in hand. "Are you okay? I didn't mean to startle you!"

"It's okay!" Misti felt both pain and elation.

Alex set the coffee on top of the locker and looked over her hand. His fingers were warm from holding their drinks.

"Doesn't look broken; might bruise. You should say that you punched someone. Give yourself some street cred."

Misti rolled her eyes, taking her hand back and retrieving her things from her locker. "Just don't sneak up on me again." Misti closed the door.

"Who *were* you talking to?" Alex said as they walked to her first class.

"What? Oh, no one. Just myself. I do that sometimes." Yes, Misti, tell people that. That will make you sound not crazy.

"I do that too, but usually in my car, not in a hallway where anyone can hear."

Despite their conversation the day before, Alex seemed intent on remaining her friend and even okay with it. Amber and Sarah didn't believe her when she assured them they were just friends. But she didn't really care. For the first time in a long time, Misti was feeling like this was a place she could be herself.

On their way from her locker, Misti was overcome with the desire to tell him everything, from the moving spinning lock, the face in the mirror and the diary. But she stopped. He had accepted one part of her; would he accept another?

At home, Misti quickly made a snack before hurrying up to her room. She sat on the bed with her chips and the diary.

October 20, 2000

He wants me to meet him again. Today, he told me he couldn't wait to see me later. We've been writing notes back and forth for the past few days, leaving them in places that no one would notice. That was his idea. How cute is that?? It has been so exciting. I agreed to sneak out again tomorrow night. I couldn't go tonight. Brian is taking me to the movies. I wanted to end things with him for real this time but H thinks it would better if I kept seeing him. It helps divert suspicion.

Hanging out with Brian now is a chore. I used to be so in love with him, but now that I've spent time with an actual man, I just know that he is not the one for me.

I almost told Shannon today. I could tell she knows something is up, so I will have to come up with something to make her understand why I've been so secretive lately. But she's been acting differently too. Maybe she knows?

Misti wondered who this mysterious H was. And the notes being left where no one would suspect? Was this a teacher?

November 13, 2000

Things with H are going so well. I went to see him after school and we locked the door and made out for like 20 minutes. I straddled him and I could tell that he was really ready to go farther.

But I know that I'm not there yet. I made up an excuse that I needed to get home.

Brian wants to know where I disappear after school. He called here all upset, and we got into a pretty serious fight. I know that I'm supposed to be "dating" him but I really don't know how long I am going to be able to keep up this charade.

I told Shannon that I was thinking about breaking up with Brian and she assumed that is why I was so distracted. I told her that I think I am finally just done with him. She didn't seem to believe me. If only she knew!

Misti read on, the diary entries getting farther and farther apart. Lily's relationship with H seemed to grow steamier with every entry.

December 28, 2000

I can't believe it. I finally lost my virginity! I always figured it would be to Brian, but it wasn't. I gave it to a real man! I told my parents I was staying over at Shannon's and told Brian and Shannon that I was sick and not to call. Then I just went straight over to his house. He cooked me dinner and even gave me a little wine. The food was okay, and the wine wasn't my favorite. But it made me feel so grown-up! Then he turned down the lights and lit some candles. We slow-danced in the living room and he told me how beautiful I was, how he was so happy that I was finally in his arms, in his home. He told me his Christmas wish had been to be with me. That the two weeks of no school had been the biggest fear of his life because he wouldn't be able to see me.

We were kissing and then the next thing I know, my clothes are off and so are his. Then it happened.

I'm not sure what I expected, but it wasn't that.

Maybe next time it will be better.

He was a teacher. Misti closed the diary. How could someone fall in love with a teacher? She thought about her two male teachers and shuddered. They were old, cranky and not attractive in the least. Misti felt sorry for Lily. She had fallen into the trap of a terrible man.

Misti wanted to keep reading, but she didn't want to see what happened. Because she knew it would not be a happy ending.

Misti lifted her mattress and gently placed the diary on the box spring. She didn't need to know what happened right now.

Eleven

The Fair

On Friday, Misti found herself in Art class sitting with Alex but not Amber. Amber had left school early to go to the county fair. She was showing one of her dogs.

"What are you doing this weekend?" Alex was working on a new piece, a guitar covered in flames and birds.

"I'm going to apply for some jobs." Misti was excited about this. She had been a little bored with what people referred to as normal. "What about you?"

"Nothing too exciting. My parents are out of town and a couple friends of mine are going to spend the weekend with me. We'll probably play games all weekend."

"Amber invited me to come watch her show her dog. You should come."

Wow, Misti. Turn the guy down one day and invite him out another. "When is it?"

"Saturday around 4. But there's a carnival with some rides and things. Sarah and Amber wanted to do that after." Good, let him know that it is a group of people. Not just you. Don't lead him on.

"Yeah, that could be fun." He grinned and pulled out his phone.

Misti perked up and then wondered if Amber would mind Alex showing up. She hadn't invited him. Misti didn't really want to go but this was a way to avoid the football game and the party. Penny was still going and Misti wanted to tell her how horrible an idea that was. But she and Penny weren't on speaking terms again. Besides, she had just heard rumors. The party was probably not going to be that crazy.

The bell rang and Misti walked with Alex to her locker.

Nothing odd had happened since seeing the morning after face in the mirror and getting the diary, but she held her breath every time she opened her locker. Nothing this time. Her books, lunch pail, and jacket were exactly where she had left them.

"Will you need a ride this weekend?"

"Maybe. My uncle can probably get me there but I'll need a ride home."

Alex agreed. "You can always text me if you need a ride."

Misti noticed people in the hall stopping and staring at them. What was everyone's fascination with her knowing Alex?

"Okay, I will."

They walked out together. It was nice of Alex to see if Penny had ditched her or not.

"See you tomorrow?" He looked at her hopefully. She nodded, and he turned and walked away again.

"What are you guys doing tomorrow?" Penny asked. Chloe was next to her. She was coming over today, to work on "yearbook" stuff, which meant planning their outfits for the party.

"We're going to see a friend show her dog and then hit up a carnival at the fair."

"Does this mean you aren't going to the game?"

"Probably."

"Oh, well. I didn't think football was really your thing, anyway." Penny didn't even try to hide how happy she was.

Uncle Bill and Aunt Mary were going to the fair with some friends so she would have a ride there.

On Saturday morning, Misti woke early and Aunt Mary dropped her off downtown. Misti applied to five places: The Blackwood Coffee shop, The Blackwood Bistro, The Blackwood Gift Shop, the Blackwood Ice Cream Parlor, and a chiropractor office called 100% Chiropractic. The coffee shop interviewed her on the spot. When she said she would like to work weekends, her interviewer looked ready to explode with excitement.

"I would hire you right now, but I have to check with the owner!" The peppy manager named Abigial had dark curly hair with beautiful skin and brown eyes. "Do you think you could start next weekend?"

Misti left with a free coffee for her aunt.

"Congratulations, honey! That's great news!" Her aunt gave her a half hug over the center console and accepted the coffee.

It was almost noon when they returned home. Uncle Bill was freshly awake and watching college football. He offered her congratulations.

"I don't officially have it yet. But it seems promising." Misti was hopeful. Of all the places she looked at, this one seemed to fit her the best. She would work Saturdays and Sundays only, opening at 6am and working until 2pm. Things were looking up.

"Penny and Chloe went out to lunch. They just woke up," Uncle Bill reported to his wife. Misti was helping putting away the groceries that her aunt had picked up while she applied for the jobs. "They're still insisting on going to the football game tonight, even though the boys stand no chance of winning."

"Well, I'm sure they go more for the boys than the winning part. You would call them fair-weather fans if they only went when they were winning." Aunt Mary winked at Misti.

"The boys aspect upsets me more than the fair-weather-fan part," Uncle Bill sighed.

Misti settled on a nice pair of boots she had bought last weekend with her aunt, a new sweater and jeans. She wore a jacket and a scarf and anxiously sat in the backseat as her uncle drove them to the park. Penny and Chloe had returned all ruffled and carrying a few shopping bags just before 3.

"Sure you don't want to go to the game?" Penny asked her. A complete change of attitude from the afternoon before. Penny seemed nervous. Misti wondered if she was her way out of going to the party.

"No, I'm good. Looking forward to the fair."

Misti had settled on keeping things civil with her cousin and only spoke to her when she started the conversation. It was a surprise to them both when Misti stopped by her room on her way down the stairs.

"You can call me if you need to tonight, you know."

Penny stared at her. Chloe was in the bathroom.

"You can't drive," Penny blushed, recognizing her comment.

"I'd find a way, if you needed me."

The cousins stared at each other, the ice melting a little.

"I'll be okay." Penny did not look or sound as confident as she usually did. "Thanks."

The bathroom door opened and Misti hurried down the stairs.

Misti pushed the conversation out of her mind as they parked. Penny was not her problem. She had spent her life taking care of someone else and cleaning up after their mistakes. Now she wanted to see what it was like to just have fun and not worry what sort of disaster was waiting for her when she got back.

"Here's some money." Uncle Bill passed her a couple bills folded together. "You can pay me back later." He winked and Misti knew he would never take her money even if she tried to give it to him.

"Remember, text me when you find your friends, and be home by midnight." Aunt Mary had told her this three times since leaving the house. Misti nodded and jumped out of the car. She was supposed to meet Sarah by the gate.

"Misti!" She wasn't even out of the parking lot. She turned and found Sarah running towards her, a multicolor bag draped over her shoulder, a brown suede jacket with fringes and black pants on. "Hey! That was easy!"

Misti turned and waved at her aunt and uncle, who she knew were watching. They were both smiling and waved back. Her phone chirped and Misti saw a message from Aunt Mary. "Have fun, be safe!"

Sarah seemed to know exactly where the arena where Amber was showing her dog was. They found her, sitting with her dog, dressed in blue jeans and a flannel, looking uncharacteristically nervous. Her dog, an Australian Shepherd, sat alert next to her, his blue eyes taking them in, wagging his tail.

"You guys came!" Amber jumped up.

"You asked us to!" Sarah hugged her friend and pet the dog. Misti smiled.

"I'm on in fifteen minutes. This is the finals. If I win, this will look so good on my resume for college."

Sarah, the future vet, seemed more interested in the dog than her friend.

"You are amazing as is. Any of your colleges will be lucky to have you." Misti tried to reassure her. It must have worked because Amber smiled and relaxed a little.

"We'll see you after the show!"

Sarah and Misti went to the stands and found a spot near the back. Amber was standing by the gate when Alex appeared, waving at them and taking the steps two at a time, trailed by the beautiful girl from the football game and another boy. Misti recognized the boy from her math class. The skinny kid who wore a lot of heavy metal band t-shirts.

"What's he doing here?" Sarah whispered.

"I invited him. I didn't think he would actually come."

"Hey guys! This is Emily and Sam. Guys, this is Misti and Sarah. Amber is down in the arena."

Misti hadn't seen Emily at school besides the football game. Typical boys, she thought. Everyone had convinced her that he was into her and she had spent days thinking about it. She even told him she wasn't interested. Maybe he just wanted to be friends. Because here he is again, with her. Misti smiled at the beautiful girl who waved at her, unable to say much over the crowd and announcer. Alex said next to her, the two bending together. Emily whispered something to Alex, who had to bend over to hear. He smiled at her. Misti forced herself to watch the dog show.

The dog show consisted of an agility course. Amber brought her dog out into the arena and took him off the leash. She ran alongside him, giving him hand signals to run through poles, jump over little fences, run a tube, run up a plank and back down. Misti and Amber cheered for their friend. Judging by the crowd reaction, she had done really well.

Misti was glad she had the distraction of the show. Who was this Emily girl? And how could Alex be interested in her when he was clearly hanging out with Emily?

"Emily, where do you go to school?" Sarah asked, leaning towards the beautiful girl with big eyes. The judges were discussing the results and Amber stood nervously with her dog and the other contestants. Misti waved at her but Amber did not see. Alex sat on her other side, chatting with Sam about something called Black Ops.

"I go online," she shrugged, smiling at Sarah. "Real school just wasn't my thing."

Sarah smiled back and the discussion was interrupted by the announcer coming back on. Third place went to a boy and his beagle. Second place went to a young girl and her lab. And first place went to Amber. Misti and the others stood up, making the same amount of noise that the fans at the football game were probably making.

"I would kill for a funnel cake!" Sarah said. They had been waiting in line for fifteen minutes. They had found Amber with her family after the show and congratulated her with hugs and high fives. Amber's parents looked meekly at them, smiling with pride at their daughter. They took Max, the Aussie, home for their daughter so she could celebrate her victory with her friends.

"Could this line move any slower?" Emily was standing with Sarah. They had been lost in conversation for most of the wait.

"I want a deep fried twinkie!" Sam announced. The group finally ordered, and then had to wait another five minutes for their food. Misti and Amber split a funnel cake covered in strawberries. Emily and Sarah split an original.

Misti found herself lost in a moment she had never thought she would be in. She was laughing at powdered sugar noses and dipping funnel cake into hot chocolate. There was no pressure; no worrying about what would happen next or tomorrow.

"Want some?" Alex sat next to her on the bench, offering her a bite of his deep fried ice cream. He fed it to her on the spoon he had been using. It was a wonderful combination of hot and cold, crispy and smooth. Better than the funnel cake.

"That's so good!"

Alex smiled.

The sound of the carousel and the shouting of the carnival game workers and the sounds of the crowd all faded as Misti looked at him. Maybe, just maybe, she could trust this one and experience another few teenage moments with him. Then, just like in the movies, the sound came crashing back over her when Emily, who was probably a pixie from a magical land, appeared from behind Alex and whispered something in his ear.

Just kidding. Misti stood up and threw away her cup. There would be no experiencing things with him. She needed to keep reminding herself that this was all temporary.

"Can we go on the carousel now?" Sarah said, heading for it already. The group followed, Emily flittering ahead with Sarah. Sam walked with Amber, who looked at him with utter horror.

"I'm glad you liked it." Alex fell into step with Misti.

The rest of the night went by pretty quickly. Alex and Misti challenged each other on a basketball hoop game and Misti won. Then they all rode a teacup, the boys spinning them as fast as they could go. They played a ring toss and won Amber a goldfish. By 11, the crowd was thinning. Amber announced she needed to get home; she had a massive paper to write the next day. Sarah offered to walk her to her car, and the two left, hugging everyone before they left and walking arm in arm.

"Do you still need a ride?" Alex asked. Misti checked her phone. Her aunt and uncle had texted that they had left around 8:30 but to call if she needed a ride.

"If you wouldn't mind," Misti said, not wanting to be alone with him and wishing she had asked Sarah instead.

"No problem." Misti, Alex, Sam, and Emily all walked towards the nearly empty parking lot.

Misti followed Emily and Alex. They were talking together. Misti could not make out what they were saying. Sam was on his phone, eating some popcorn.

"See you later, kid," Emily said, hugging Alex tightly and giving him a quick kiss on the cheek. "It was nice to see you again! Bye, Sam!" Emily climbed into a little car that hummed to life before driving away.

"Emily is nice," Misti said, walking with Alex towards his car.

"Yea, she is."

There was an awkward pause as Alex opened the passenger door for her. Misti stepped in, thanking him. They drove out of the lot, music playing quietly on the radio. Misti was racking her brain for something to cut the tension. Sam was sitting in the back, still looking at his phone. Her phone ringing broke the silence. Misti looked. It was Penny. Fear gripped her chest.

"Hey, what's up?"

"Have you gotten home yet?"

"No, Alex is taking me there now."

"Can you come get me?"

Twelve

The Rescue

⬯⬯⬯

Alex didn't require any more explanation than Misti saying she needed to go get Penny from the party. They got to the house out in the country about fifteen minutes later. There were about twenty cars all lined up in the driveway.

Misti saw Penny sitting on the porch. Alex pulled up and Misti jumped out, jogging up the steps. As her boots hit the porch, a familiar figure materialized in the door frame.

"Misti! So glad you could make it!" Tony opened the door for her. Misti ignored him, moving to Penny. She was wasted, and she had been crying. Misti pulled her to her feet and grabbed her purse. Her usually strong and tall cousin's knees sagged and Misti wasn't tall enough to support her well. She grit her teeth and held her up. Penny felt like a rag doll and a sack of flour all rolled into one.

"Hey, what's the rush? Come inside." Tony grabbed Misti's arm, but she shook him off.

"No, we're leaving."

Tony frowned. "I think that apology was a meaningless one."

104

Misti rolled her eyes at him. Tony took a step towards her but halted when Alex and Sam appeared.

"Need help?" Alex said. "Hey, Tony."

"Alex." Tony took two steps back. For the first time since meeting him, Misti saw Tony look intimidated by someone. She looked at Alex, who didn't seem to notice; he was focusing on her. Sam stood a little behind Alex, balancing on the balls of his feet, his hands closed in tight fists. For the first time that night, she did not see his cellphone.

"Penny, is Chloe here too?"

As if summoned, Chloe jumped out of the house shrieking with laughter. "Tony! Come back inside! The game is getting so good!" She quit when she saw Misti holding up Penny. "Oops!" She spun and ran back in, howling like a hyena.

"Chloe is fine," Tony said.

Alex gently lifted Penny's other arm over his shoulder and helped Misti get her into his car. Misti fished out the keys from Penny's purse.

"I can't drive," Misti said.

"I'll follow you. Which one is it?" Sam took the keys without hesitation.

Misti pointed to Penny's little sedan and climbed into the backseat of Alex's car with Penny. Alex drove faster than he should. They were going to be home just before midnight.

"Dad is gonna be so mad!" Penny told Misti, her eyes welling with tears. Misti was plotting in her head. How could they get into the house without Uncle Bill knowing?

Alex parked on the street in front of the house and Sam pulled into the driveway. Misti took the keys from him and thanked them both.

"Do you need help?" Alex said. Misti hated that he expressed so much concern. It made her appreciate him more.

"No; not my first drunk girl experience," Misti said. Alex cocked his head in bewilderment. Misti could have told him how she learned to mix drinks when she was ten but decided it was not the time. Penny was able to walk better but still leaned on Misti. They entered the house and Misti waved to Alex and Sam before shutting the door.

The TV was on and Penny leaned against the frame of the door waiting. "No covering for me this time." Penny glanced at her with wet eyes. But no voice came. Misti slipped off her boots and helped Penny stumble out of her heels. She peeped around the corner and saw Uncle Bill asleep on the couch. A small miracle. Misti hurried Penny upstairs, easing her out of her clothes. Penny was asleep before Misti was out of the room.

Misti went back downstairs, checking the time. It was just after midnight.

"Uncle Bill?" she said, touching his shoulder. Uncle Bill jerked awake, staring at her. "Hey, sorry. Just wanted to let you know I'm home."

"Penny?" he asked. His voice was half asleep.

"She must have gotten in before me. Her car is here. Want me to go check?"

Uncle Bill shook his head and laid back down. "Thanks for letting me know."

Misti couldn't sleep once she got to her room. She changed into pjs and climbed into bed, taking out her journal.

Dear J,

Tonight was another first. I got to spend time with a lot of fun people and experience a small town fair. Yes, it was exactly like those cheesy movies.

The thing with Alex, I can tell that if I let myself, I could really fall for him. I have never, ever said that about someone, but there is just something about him. Mom would say it was his aura or his smell or something stupid like that. She would also be so happy that I was interested in someone. Well, sticking with experiencing the life of a true teenager, he already has a girlfriend. Emily. And she is like an actual fairy. She is so slim and perfect. She has big eyes and perfect teeth and silky hair.

Nothing like me.

I'm glad Penny called me. I should have tried to stop her from going. I don't think Chloe is the best friend that she thinks she is.

Also, hopefully I have a job starting next Saturday! It would be nice to have my own money. Hopefully Sarah and Amber want to keep hanging out.

Overall, J, this place isn't that bad.

Misti woke to light tapping on her door. Looking at the clock, she was surprised to see it was after 9. J was on the bed next to her and the pen tucked inside. She must have dozed off while writing.

"Come in," she said, pushing herself up. Penny stepped into the room. Her hair was pulled back into a messy ponytail, her face was pale, and she had to touch the corner of the dresser, focusing hard. Misti recognized the signs of a bad hangover. She wondered if her aunt and uncle would too.

"Thanks for coming last night." Penny's voice was hoarse. "Things got a little crazy."

"You're welcome." Misti pulled her knees up to her chest and tucked J under the pillow.

"I don't remember much after calling you, and before that was a blur. I think I drank too much."

Misti nodded.

"Alex was with me, and his friend, Sam. Sam drove your car home, you rode with me and Alex. Tony tried to stop me from taking you."

Penny sat on the edge of the bed, leaning against the frame.

"I had never drunk before. I mean, outside the glass of eggnog Mom let me try last Christmas and sips of beer I took from Dad." She took a deep breath in and Misti wondered if she would puke; she was looking a little green. "Tony and Chloe convinced me to take a shot, and Tony made me have this red drink. It tasted horrible, but…" Tears formed in Penny's eyes. "I just wanted him to not think I was an absolute loser."

"Chloe looked like she was having fun," Misti said, retrieving tissues off the dresser. Penny blew her nose.

"Yeah, she drinks all the time. Did you know she went to that party last weekend? Tony picked her up after we dropped her off." Tears formed in her eyes again. "And last night I found out that Chloe and Tony hooked up."

Misti sat down next to Penny and let her cousin cry on her shoulder. Comforting someone was something Misti did well.

"No offense, but Chloe seems like a shit friend."

"I know. Well, I know now. But she spent the entire week telling me that Tony was not talking to me because of you. After you apologized, he was still so distant. We used to text, like, constantly. And now, I know it wasn't because of you. Chloe has been lying to me." Penny blew her nose again.

"I don't know if you want to hear this, but honestly, Tony is a douche. You deserve someone so much better than him. I mean, have you ever actually listened to the way he talks?"

Penny let out a little laugh, breaking up the tears.

"I know, but, I've had a crush on him since, like, the seventh grade. And this year, he started to notice me. I was hoping we'd be more than just talking soon. He told me so many times in text how much he wanted me."

"Did he ever say it in person?"

"Well, no. But we were always around other people and he said he's really shy."

Misti never would have used the word 'shy' to describe Tony.

"It doesn't matter now; I'm totally over him. And I'm so mad at Chloe.

She and I have been best friends for, like, five years. She never told me she liked Tony. Like, if she had, I would have never spent so much time on him." Misti doubted that. Chloe probably didn't like Tony. "I think I'm more upset about losing my best friend than anything."

Misti understood that. Once she and her mother had stayed in an apartment for almost six months. Misti was younger, still in elementary school, and she hadn't learned that the lifestyle she had was not normal. There was a little girl across the hall from them and they would spend hours playing in the hall with their toys. Looking back, Misti knew now that she was just as poor as her. She lived with her mom and her mom's father. Her grandfather, Papi, would tell them stories at night. Misti often stayed the night.

It was just after Christmas but Misti was back in school. She and the girl—Misti couldn't remember her name anymore—were being walked home by Papi. Misti had her Christmas present with her. It was a brand new Barbie. It was the only gift she got that year, and she remembered being so excited that she had to cut her out of the box. The girl across the hall had gotten one too, but her Barbie was a doctor and Misti's just had a nice dress.

They were talking to each other with their Barbies and heading up the steps when Misti's mother came out carrying their things. She was loading a cab, and she told Misti to get in, gripping her arm roughly and shoving her into the car.

Misti didn't get to say goodbye.

She cried for the rest of the day, even after her mother threatened to smack her. And so her mother smacked her. So she just cried without making a sound.

Instead of telling her cousin she knew how she felt, Misti rubbed her back and let her cry.

After about twenty minutes, Penny said she was going to shower. Misti hoped that would clean her up enough to get by as just tired. She didn't think her aunt and uncle would go easy on their daughter.

"Everything okay?" Aunt Mary asked her when Misti sat at the bar. Aunt Mary was stacking pancakes. She must have heard Penny crying.

"Yeah, just some drama." Misti shrugged. Aunt Mary looked at her, wanting more, but Misti was feeling protective of her cousin again. Maybe she would get something in return this time.

Misti was chewing her fourth pancake when Penny appeared, hair still wet but looking normal otherwise besides her wet eyes. She must have continued crying in the shower.

"Oh, baby, what is it?" Aunt Mary hurried to her daughter and wrapped her in a hug. Penny wept. Penny told her about Chloe and Tony. A variant of Tony and Chloe. She left out the parties and the drinking and the sex.

"I'm so, so sorry, baby. That is just horrible. I would never have thought Chloe capable of doing that." Aunt Mary smoothed her hair. Uncle Bill wandered in and looked startled to see his wife holding their daughter. She waved him off, pointing to the pancakes hidden under a towel. Uncle Bill shrugged and joined Misti at the counter. He nodded his head towards them, raising his eyebrows.

"Boy drama. Best friend drama." Misti shrugged.

"Do I need to go find a boy and teach him a lesson?" Uncle Bill asked, piling his pancakes on his plate.

"Oh, Dad," Penny pulled away from her mother for a moment. "That would be like the worst thing you could do!" But she was smiling a little.

"I know a lot of places to hide bodies," he said. Aunt Mary shook her head, smiling.

Plotting murder over pancakes. Misti liked it.

Misti's phone began to ring just as she stacked the last dish in the dishwasher.

"Hello, Misti? This is Abigail, from Blackwood Cafe. Just got done talking to the owner and you're good to go! Are you still interested?"

"Yes! Of course!" Her aunt and uncle stared at her, tilting their heads.

"Awesome! Can you swing by sometime this week, maybe Wednesday or Thursday to fill out the new employee paperwork?" Misti agreed and confirmed she would be there Thursday.

"I can take you," Penny said. "Maybe I can get a free coffee while I wait?"

Misti smiled at Penny. Worth protecting her again.

"She can't use perks for a job she doesn't have yet!" Aunt Mary scolded her.

Misti and Penny giggled together. Misti went to her room, feeling relieved for the first time. She had a job, she had friends, she was back on good terms with her cousin. The only complication was a boy. And a possibly haunted locker. Misti pulled out the diary, staring at the leather cover in her hands, twisting the ribbon at the end around her finger. Nothing odd had happened since seeing Lily earlier in the week.

"You've been under a lot of stress. There has been a ton of change. You imagined it. And the other things are elaborate pranks being done by other kids because you're the new girl and they're trying to scare you." Misti tucked the diary back under her bed.

Thursday afternoon, she and Penny headed to the cafe where Misti would be working. Penny came inside with her and took over a corner booth, ordering a decaf soy no sugar something or another. Misti ordered a tea.

She filled out her paperwork, while the same peppy manager, Abigail, filled her in on what her role would be.

"First, we will train you on the register. Then you will learn how to make the coffee. Most people are simple, only ordering off the menu.

But every once in a while, you get someone who wants something very specific." Abigail and Misti looked over at Penny, who was sipping her drink and looking at something on her phone. Misti imagined that she was trying to be very adult right in that moment.

"Awesome! I just want to thank you for giving me the chance."

"No problem. Most of my staff never want to work weekends and will call off if I schedule them. This is a small town but we have a little rush on Saturday right before grocery shopping time and on Sunday after church. Other than that, weekends are slow."

Misti learned that her schedule would be Saturday from 6am to 2pm. She would earn minimum wage with a chance of a small raise in 90 days. She would split the tip jar with whoever else worked that day.

"Most of the time, you'll work with me. I like the weekends and I enjoy having Monday and Tuesday off. Sometimes you'll have to work with Nevaeh. She is another manager, but she works weekdays only unless I'm on vacation or sick." Abigail gave Misti a big hug as they stood to leave. "I am so excited to have you join our family."

"I think Misti needs to learn to drive," Uncle Bill announced at the dinner table that night. Misti looked at him, a fork of spaghetti only halfway to her mouth. Aunt Mary stared at him, glaring. This must have been a conversation they had already had and Uncle Bill had not listened to what they had decided.

"I don't mind driving her!" Aunt Mary said. "I'm up that early, anyway!"

"I know that! I'm just saying that it's a skill everyone needs and she might as well learn now!"

"Maybe she doesn't want to learn."

Penny and Misti looked at each other and Penny rolled her eyes. They had discussed on the drive home how Penny hated when her parents talked about her as if she wasn't in the room. And now they were doing it to Misti.

"I could learn," Misti said. "If you don't mind teaching me."

"Of course not!" Uncle Bill flashed a told-you-so grin at Aunt Mary before resuming his meal.

"You don't have to if you don't want to."

"I know. I think it will be good for me. I mean, I can't rely on other people to drive me around for the rest of my life, can I?"

Thirteen

The First Day

Misti woke a minute before her alarm. She lay still, listening to the stillness of the house. Even though she had been with her aunt and uncle for a short time, she was comfortable. This was the safest she had been in a long time. She had never really let herself think about that in the places she lived with her mother but she knew she always slept a little lighter, just in case. Misti pushed back the blankets and got up, silencing the alarm before it could do its job. She dressed in the clothes she had laid out the night before: a pair of darker jeans and a T-shirt with the Blackwood Coffee logo on it. She brushed and braided her hair before putting on makeup.

She quietly made her way down the stairs and fixed herself a small breakfast of cereal and one piece of toast. She was rinsing her bowl when Aunt Mary appeared.

"Good morning!"

"Morning!" They both spoke in hushed tones despite knowing that nothing short of a hurricane would wake Penny and her father right now.

It was thirty-five minutes after five when they pulled out of the driveway. The lights in town were flashing red and they only met one other car as they drove downtown. Aunt Mary pulled in front and smiled at Misti.

"I'm so proud of you, Misti."

Misti glanced over at her, hand frozen on the handle of the SUV. No one had ever said those words to her before.

"You've handled this whole thing—your mother, the move, new place to live—with such grace. You've made friends, you got a job." Aunt Mary looked at the coffee shop. "I don't think I would have been able to do that."

"You and Uncle Bill and Penny have all made it so I could."

Aunt Mary's eyes were shining. Although they were both morning people, it was too early for this sort of emotion.

"Have a good day! I'll pick you up at 2:00?" Misti nodded and jumped out of the car, hurrying to the door. Abigail had to unlock it for her.

"Morning, morning, morning!" the manager sang to her. Misti wondered if she was related to her aunt. She took the morning person thing to a new level. "Are you ready for your first day?"

Misti nodded. She had always been a fast learner, and by the end of the day Abigail trusted her on the register and had started teaching her how to make a few drinks. The day itself went very quickly. The coffee shop had one "rush" of fifteen people. But of what Misti could tell; none of them were actually in a hurry. The customers looked to be mostly young mothers, babies strapped to their chests or in strollers. They all sat and chatted. Some were clearly gossiping about another woman who sat in the corner with a man that Misti took not to be her husband.

They always stopped talking when Misti came to check on them.

"You're new?" one of them asked. She had dark brown eyes and a crooked nose. Her makeup was caked on and although her face was smooth and flawless, Misti could not say she was attractive.

"Yes, it's my first day."

"Did you just move here?"

"I did. Can I get you anything else?"

"No, that's okay." The woman eyed her up and down.

"Misti!" Abigail called from behind the counter. Misti picked up a few more coffee cups on her way back.

"I would avoid talking to that woman." Abigail murmured, helping her set the dishes in the dishwasher.

"Who is she?"

"Shannon Turner. She's a piece of work." Abigail stopped herself. "I shouldn't speak poorly of paying customers. She comes here almost every day and posts my designs in her lattes to her Instagram. People from out of town have stopped here because of that. But I've had to watch YouTube videos at night and practice how to do more than circles," Abigail sighed.

"Does she have a son—Alex?"

"Stepson. Do you know Alex?"

"Yeah, he's a friend." Abigail raised ane eybrow, a smile on her lips. "A friend?"

Misti just nodded and was thankful for the bell that had just rung alerting them to a new customer.

"Uh, hello, miss, we would like to order some coffee please."

Misti smiled. Amber and Sarah grinned at her.

"Hey, guys," she said. "What can we make you?"

"Do you have anything that doesn't taste like coffee?" Sarah asked, looking over the menu.

"I'll take a jasmine tea," Amber said.

"We have frappes. Those don't have much coffee in them. But they are iced."

Sarah said she would try one of those and Misti rang them up. Amber paid and her two friends gave her the thumbs up.

"We're actually meeting Emily here in a few minutes. Amber is our escort." Misti made a face. Why were they suddenly friends with Emily?

"I am not! It was my idea to come here like two days ago. You invited Emily along."

Misti poured hot water over the tea bag into a cup for Amber before going over to observe Abigail as she made the frappe. It seemed pretty simple.

Her friends were still bickering as they made their way to a table. Misti wiped down the counter, aware that Shannon was watching her. Alex never really talked about his stepmom. Misti was under the impression that it was just him and his father.

Emily came in about ten minutes later, confidently coming up to the counter to order a latte with two pumps of caramel, one pump of vanilla, and an extra shot of espresso. Misti made it under the supervision of Abigail.

"Are you coming out tonight?" Emily asked her, dropping a dollar in the tip jar that was almost overflowing.

"Maybe. I have to work early tomorrow." Misti was not keen on the idea of watching Alex and his girlfriend whisper into each others ears.

Emily nodded and went to sit with Sarah and Amber, who had made themselves at home on the couch in the corner. Misti watched as Emily sat next to Sarah and gave her a kiss and hooked her fingers through Sarah's.. She knew her mouth had dropped open. Amber looked at Misti, titled her head in confusion and confused herself.

"What's wrong?" Amber asked, busying herself at the coffee station, looking through the sugars.

"I thought Emily was dating Alex?"

"Emily? No. She and Sarah have been dating since the fair. Emily and Alex are just friends. Sarah doesn't remember her, because she is older than us. But I remember her." Amber glanced over her shoulder at the new couple lost in conversation. "It was sophomore year. Emily was a junior and the first openly gay person at our school. Tony, looking to make a name for himself, was being a total douche. He was always harrassing her. Finally, at lunch, Alex told him to knock it off. Tony shoved him, Alex knocked him out. One punch and down." Amber had a little smile on her lips. "Everyone cheered. It was a good fight! Well, good not fight. Anyway, Emily transferred to online school and remained friends with Alex." Amber selected a sugar, smirked at Misti and said, "So, yeah. Not dating Alex." Misti stood rag in her hand, watching Amber join her two friends.

At one thirty, Penny, Aunt Mary, and Uncle Bill all entered.

"Abigail, you remember my cousin? This is my Aunt Mary and my Uncle Bill." Abigail gushed about how well Misti was doing. Misti tried to hide a blush while she poured her uncle his black coffee, got her aunt a cappuccino, and made Penny her complicated drink, only needing Abigail's help once. Her family took their drinks and sat at a table by a window. Penny got her phone out and Uncle Bill and Aunt Mary looked out the window, pointing out things to each other.

"I didn't know I would get a crowd by hiring you," Abigail grinned at her. "Didn't you just move here? How are you so popular already?"

"Three of them are family, so that doesn't count."

"A paying customer is a paying customer." Abigail grinned at her before disappearing in the back.

Misti finished her shift and learned how to close. Aunt Mary told her that they would be across the street at the craft store when she was done. Amber, Sarah, and Emily all begged her to come out with them tonight.

"It will be so much fun!" Emily said, jumping up and down on the balls of her feet. Misti sighed and agreed to go.

"See you there!" The girls all chimed, leaving Misti to lock the door.

Misti got a little over twenty dollars in tips.

"Same time, same channel tomorrow!" Abigail told her.

"See you then!" Misti knew she was smiling. It felt good to be working again and felt even better to have her own money. She knew her uncle didn't care, but she felt guilty any time he slipped her some. Misti found her uncle sitting on a bench outside the craft store.

"Not your scene?" Misti sat with him.

"Doilies and handmade candles? Not really. I always feel like a bull in a china shop in there. How was your first day?"

"It went really well. I like it in there." She showed him the twenty in tips and he whistled.

"That's pretty good for a quiet little coffee shop."

Uncle Bill did not push it. They sat in silence, letting the sun warm their faces while their legs froze from the slight breeze blowing around them. The door opened behind them and Aunt Mary emerged, carrying a couple bags. Penny followed her, carrying one more.

"What's the damage?"

"It isn't that bad. We just got a few things for Christmas!" Aunt Mary scolded. Uncle Bill took her bags from her and led the way to the car. In the car, Penny showed Misti the adult coloring book she had bought.

"It might help me relax a little. Help me destress."

"Looks fun!" It was a Christmas-themed one and there were hundreds of tiny lines to fill in. Misti could see herself spending days on one picture, making sure the shading was correct. It would not be relaxing for her.

Aunt Mary wanted a full report on her first day, asking questions about customers and coffees and how her feet felt and if she needed anything clothes-wise for work.

"Mary, she had a long day. She said it was good. She gave you some detail. If you want to see who goes there, sit in there and watch."

At home, Misti took a short nap. She was a morning person but learning a new task, despite it not being stressful, was still exhausting. She woke an hour later to her phone chiming. It was Alex, wanting to know about her first day. It made her smile.

It was good! Learning some new skills, saw some people. Made 20 bucks in tips.

She got out of bed.

Awesome! I guess you are buying tonight! Bowling with the others?

Misti thought about it while she combed her hair.

Sure! But I have to be back early. I work again tomorrow.

Career woman! Sounds good. I'll pick you up at 7?

Misti went downstairs and found football on the TV. Her aunt was in the kitchen looking over a cookbook.

"Is it alright if I go bowling with a few friends tonight? I'll be back early for work."

"Of course!"

Misti texted Alex back that that would work and went back upstairs. She noticed Penny's door propped open and peaked inside. She was sitting at her desk, her new book in front of her. But it wasn't open.

She was staring at the wall. Misti knocked on her door.

"Hey! What are your plans for tonight?"

"Oh, well, the team is out of town and we just submitted some spreads so no yearbook tasks. Probably just stay home, watch a movie with Mom and Dad."

"Want to go bowling?"

Fourteen

Normality

⁓

"I'm so bad at this!" Amber said, watching her ball slowly roll down the aisle, casually moving to the right, teetering on the edge for a moment then crashing into the gutter just before the pins.

"You need to stop throwing across your body; throw it straight," Sarah said.

Amber looked over at her. "I don't know what that means! I am throwing it straight!"

Sarah, who had her own ball, shoes, and was even sporting a bowling shirt with Blackwood Veternairy Clinic printed on the back, came over to Amber and began a little lesson.

"I'm just as awful at this, Amber!" Penny offered support. Misti's cousin was looking a lot happier than she had all week. Misti felt bad that she had not noticed how down she had been. But Penny was also rarely around her this week. Other than the rides to school and dinner time, she only saw her a few times.

Next to Penny was Sam, Alex's friend from the fair. Misti could tell that he was hanging on Penny's every word. He was about Penny's height with shaggy blond hair, a new tattoo on his arm, and dark eyes.

"You aren't that bad. She's pretty bad," Sam said.

Penny looked at him and smiled. Misti wondered if she noticed the way Sam was watching her.

"Your turn!" Alex said in her ear and Misti jumped. She had forgotten he was there. She was getting used to his presence. Not good. It didn't help that knowing Emily was out of the picture, she just lost one of her excuses for not being with him.

Misti did her best, managing to knock down seven pins. Despite her poor attempts and this being the third time she had ever been bowling and the first time in years, Misti was in fourth place. Alex and Sarah kept going back and forth on first, Sam was in second, and Emily was in third. Penny followed Misti and Amber was last.

"You seem tired." Alex had a way of talking tonight that managed to eliminate the world around them so it was just the two of them in a secure bubble.

"I got up at 5:00 this morning for work."

Alex smiled. "Let me know when you want to go; I can take you home whenever."

"Thanks." Misti felt a ripple in her chest. Whatever was happening with her and him, she was not liking it tonight. Looking over at Penny, though, she knew that she should give her a little longer out. She was laughing at Sam.

The game ended three rounds later with Sarah as the victor and Alex in a close second. Misti knew that Alex had thrown the game for Sarah. He had done it so slightly. But he missed picking up a spare that he had done all night. She didn't know how that made her feel.

"Arcade, anyone?"

Misti looked at Penny, who was hurrying away to join the others as they made their way to the arcade, then looked at her watch. It was a little after 9. Misti was hoping to be in bed soon.

"Let me take you home. I can make sure Penny gets home later. She and Sam seem to be having fun." Misti hesitated. Was that allowed? Could she just leave her?

"She'll be fine. If she survived the party last weekend, arcade games with us will be nothing."

Misti agreed and said goodbye to everyone. Penny looked a little sad but didn't say anything, also starting her goodbyes.

"Alex is coming back and he said he can give you a ride later."

Penny brightened, thanking Alex.

"I'll see you tomorrow after work?"

Penny nodded before returning to Sam, who was showing off at the basketball game.

"I met your stepmom today," Misti told Alex as he drove them towards her house.

"I bet that was pleasant." The disdain in his voice was hard to miss.

"You guys don't get along?"

Alex sighed and for the first time Misti had ever seen, he was neither happy nor calm.

"She's very full of herself, and mostly for no reason. I think my dad married her because she was the exact opposite of my mom. Most of the time, he doesn't even seem to like her."

"What happened to your mom?"

"She died, about ten years ago. Cancer."

"I'm so sorry." Misti wanted to tell him she knew what it was like to lose a mom. Although, technically, her mom was still alive. But Misti had lost her.

"It's okay. It was a long time ago. My dad married Shannon about two years after my mom died. And she is what she is." Alex paused. "Was she nice to you at least?"

"She was just trying to figure me out, I think. Another one of you

123

local yokels not used to outsiders coming in and taking your jobs."

Alex smiled again. "I'm glad you're here. You can have any of my jobs if it means you stay."

Tingles traveled up Misti's arm.

They arrived at the house and Misti had to remind herself it was still early by anyone's standards. She knew her aunt and uncle would be on the couch, watching something. Her aunt would probably be asleep.

"Thanks for understanding. I just don't want to be beyond tired on my second day."

"I get it."

Misti sat in the car, watching him watch her. She had a sudden urge to kiss him. Instead, she got out of the car and waved goodbye.

"Home early?" Uncle Bill called from the couch.

"Yeah, tired from the day. Penny stayed out with them, though. Alex said he would get her home later."

"How was bowling?"

"Good! I'm not very good."

Aunt Mary was not on the couch. She must have already gone to bed.

"Sleep tight!" Misti climbed the stairs and crawled into her bed.

She could be nothing more than friends with Alex. She had to remind herself of that. It wouldn't be fair to him. If they worked out, in a few years, when she wound up being like her mother, she didn't want him to have to go through what she did. She didn't want him lying for her, making up reasons why she wasn't where she was supposed to be, or telling neighbors that she was rehearsing for a play and that was why there were so many weird noises coming from their apartment. She didn't want him to have to take on more work to support them. Because she had done it all and knew that it made her resent her mother. It would make him resent her. And she could not stand the thought of him resenting her.

Work the next day was the same crowd of people, with a few new faces all dressed up for church. Abigail told her at the end of her shift that she would be running the store herself in no time if she kept learning like she did. She also gave Misti a book of instructions on how to make all the fancy coffees. She was supposed to study it this week and start making a few more orders next week. She also got her tips for the day, a little more than yesterday.

"People are more giving on Sunday. Especially after church."

Uncle Bill picked up Misti and started to drive home. But instead of going home, he went to the high school. The parking lot was empty. He parked in the middle of the lot and unbuckled.

"Time to learn how to drive."

It was a lot easier learning to drive than Misti thought it might be. Uncle Bill was patient, walking her through the instructions a little at a time.

"Keep your hands at 10 and 2. Use your right foot, step on the break, then put her in gear." Misti started out moving at a snail's pace. After a few minutes, she picked up speed. After about fifteen, she was driving around the lot with ease.

She couldn't drive home, but Uncle Bill told her that they would go down to the DMV this week and take the permit test.

"There's something online you can study. Penny should remember where to find it."

Penny was sitting in the living room but hurried up the stairs after Misti after she got home.

"I had such a good time last night! Thanks so much for inviting me! Sam is so sweet! He won me a little teddy bear in the arcade after you left!"

"I'm glad you had fun!" Misti said. Misti needed to do homework and study for a permit test. She also didn't want to think about last night. She had spent the last hour telling herself not to text Alex. She wanted to talk to him, see if he had any more fun last night after she left.

"Alex seemed super bummed when he got back," Penny sat on Misti's bed, ignoring the fact that Misti was taking out her pack and pulling out her books.

"That's weird. He seemed fine when he dropped me off."

"He was sad because you weren't there."

Misti sighed and looked at Penny. "You know why I can't be with him."

Penny shook her head.

"My mother was crazy. Legit crazy. She talked to herself, she suffered paranoia, she couldn't get out of bed for days and then not sleep for others. She was unwell. And I'm probably going to end up like that too. Because how could I not?"

Penny's bright face had drained of color as Misti spoke and she lowered her eyes now.

"I'm not trying to scare you. I just don't want to put anyone in the position that I was in.."

"I understand."

But Misti doubted she did.

"Do you want to talk about what happened? With your mom, I mean?"

Misti shook her head and offered a smile. She had gotten good at fake smiling. "I'm okay. Thanks, though."

Penny hung out for a few more minutes, talking about Sam and how cute he was. She showed Misti some texts that he had sent her that day. Penny told her that he was all set to go to school next year for some computer training. Right now he was a hacker.

"A hacker? Like, breaks into people's computers?"

"Yeah, well, he doesn't take people's money. He does harmless stuff. I think?" Penny frowned for just a second. She perked up, shaking off the thought of picking another bad guy. "We're just talking right now but I can see it going somewhere."

"Just talking?"

"Yeah. That means we like each other but we haven't made any commitments."

By that definition, Misti was just talking to Alex. And Amber and Sarah.

Before she left to do her own homework, Penny showed Misti where to get the permit test information and assured Misti it was super easy to pass.

"Oh and hey, can you try to be a little more quiet when you get up in the middle of the night? You scared the bejesus out of me!"

Misti tilted her head and apologized. She thought she had been quiet when she left for work that morning.

Misti spent the rest of the afternoon finishing homework and reading about driving. After an uneventful dinner and packing of lunch, Misti took a long shower and told her family good night. She was tired from the last two days and knew she would be asleep before lights out were called. But when she laid down, she found she could not sleep. She journaled for a few minutes, telling J about work and writing out the steps for the most popular drinks she could remember. But still, she could not sleep. She felt the diary, heard it whispering to her to read some more. Lily wanted her to know her story.

She got out of bed and pulled out the diary.

January 13, 2000

H didn't talk to me. He couldn't even look at me. I feel so horrible. What did I do wrong? I thought I was doing everything he wanted me to do. Ever since that night, things have been different.

Brian broke up with me again too. This is literally the worst.

January 25, 2001

H explained himself finally. He said that he could see himself falling in love with me too much and was worried about his feelings. I told him that we could keep it simple until after I graduated. I mean, that's only a few months away. And we had gotten pretty good about sneaking around. And with Brian out of the picture, it will be much easier!

I'm so relieved he is speaking with me again.

March 3, 2001

We have gotten to be experts at sneaking around. He still leaves notes for me and I leave notes for him. The play is coming up and I'm going to be the stage manager, which gives me a lot of reasons to speak with him in front of everyone. H and I have started making love more consistently and it is starting to feel good. We usually do it at his house but sometimes he wants me in the school. I'm always worried we will get caught but it never lasts very long.

March 27, 2001

I think I'm in serious trouble. I think I'm pregnant. I missed my period. I have to take a test but I'm so scared. H told me this wouldn't happen because he didn't need to wear protection. I feel like this is all my fault! I don't even know what I am going to tell people. I really wish I could talk to someone about this, but H told me that if people found out, I would be in more trouble

than he would. He would just lose his job. And they would keep us apart.
  I don't want to lose him.

April 4, 2001

I bought a test. It was positive. This is literally the worst thing that could happen.
  On top of all of this, Brian asked me to prom and before I could stop myself, I said yes. So, I'm going to prom with a guy I don't like while trying to decide if I should tell the man I love about his baby.
  I think I need to talk to Shannon about all of this. Out of everyone, she will know what to do.

April 14, 2001

I talked to Shannon a few days ago. I just started crying in her car and it all came out. I told her about H and the baby and Brian. She was so supportive. We came up with a plan to save H.
  I don't know if it is going to work, but at prom tomorrow, Brian is finally going to get to make love to me like he's been begging for. And, in a few weeks, I'm going to announce that I'm pregnant and it is his.

There were no more entries after that. Misti closed the diary and looked at the ceiling. She wondered what happened, if Brian was trapped by these girls, if he found out, if H found out.

Was Lily Banks dead? If so, when did she die and how? She assumed that the girl in her locker was Lily. Didn't someone tell her the girl that haunted the locker was killed on prom night? Did Brian kill Lily? Her eyes began to close, the weekend finally catching up to her. Mist was just about to fall asleep when she heard her door open, slowly and softly. Her Aunt coming in to check on her? Penny? She heard the footsteps moving towards her and a hand touched her arm. Misti let her eyes float open.

There was no one there.

Fifteen

Investigating

⁓᷂◊᷂⁓

At her locker the next day, Misti waited for something to happen. But there was no spinning lock and no face in the mirror. Her books and notebooks were right where she left them.

"Why do you look so disappointed?"

Misti turned to Alex. She didn't know how to explain she was upset because her locker, which she thought was haunted, hadn't done anything over the weekend to show her that it was.

"Just Monday." She closed the locker and accepted the coffee from Alex. She was looking forward to this treat from him every day.

"How was work yesterday?"

"Good! I really enjoy it. And it will be nice making money again. Maybe I can buy you coffee. And my uncle started to teach me how to drive. I go take the test on Thursday!" Misti was shocked at how excited she sounded. She had stopped looking forward to promises from the future.

"I didn't know you never learned to drive. Why not?"

Misti was quiet now. She didn't want to bring up the past.

"Never really needed to when we lived in Chicago. Trains and buses everywhere. We sold our car. There was never anywhere to park anyway." It was a little white lie. They had a car and it was taken away because the bank wanted them to make the payments. And she never would have been able to learn from her mother.

Alex nodded and Misti saw for the first time that he didn't believe her. Was he starting to wonder? Did he want more information than what Penny had offered him? Had Penny even told him anything juicy? He never asked, though. Another thing to admire about him.

The day went as all days do: class, lunch, more class, then Art. Misti realized she liked that class most not because she liked to draw but because she sat with Alex. And she laughed with Alex.

Her locker never changed. Everything stayed where it was again that day. And the next. For the next several weeks, everything continued as normal. She passed her driving test and took all the chances she could to drive. She would get her license just before graduation.

She learned all the drinks at the coffee shop and began to know the regulars. She spent her Friday and Saturday nights with Penny, Sarah, Amber, or Alex.

She was becoming more comfortable with her aunt and uncle, spending time with them on Sundays attempting to learn about football. Penny and Sam were still "just talking."

She was learning to love being a normal teenager.

During all of this, the locker remained quiet. Nothing seemed to happen.

Perhaps Lily just wanted someone to know her story.

"How are things going, Misti?"

She was back in her therapist's office. She felt she could tell him honestly that things were good. Not just good but great.

It was Christmas break and they had the next two weeks off from school. Misti and Penny had passed all their classes. Misti was going to work at the coffee house on Wednesday and Friday but spend Christmas with her family. Aunt Mary had been stressing over the meal for the past two weeks. Uncle Bill's parents were coming to town and Penny told her that Aunt Mary and Grandma Pat did not really get along.

Misti told the therapist that she was really happy. She showed him her grades—all As and a B in math because she did not do so well on the last test.

"It looks like you're really coming into your own here," he told her at the end of their session. "Have you spoken with your mother?"

Misti was taken aback by the question. Her dreams were still happening, although not as frequently, and she had not woken the house again.

"No."

"Do you want to talk to her? Would she be happy to hear about how well you're doing here?"

Misti shrugged. She knew the answer. Her mother would smile and say "that's nice, dear." And then spend the rest of the time telling her all her woes. Her mother had never really cared about her daughter.

"What are you thinking?"

Misti said nothing, turning to look at the certificates above his desk. "You don't have to defend her anymore. It's okay if you're angry with her."

"She wouldn't care," Misti told him. "She'd be upset with me."

"Why upset?"

"I don't know. But I remember once, in fifth grade, I came home with an award from school. I won it for helping out a classmate. My mother tore it up."

"How did that make you feel?"

Misti had never talked about her mother to anyone before. She felt

133

a bubble of anxiety filling her chest, a sense of betrayal.

"It's okay. You can tell me."

"I cried. And she laughed. She told me that it was a pity prize. That she and I weren't ever going to be anything. That I could trust no one but her." Misti looked at her hands. "I knew then that something was wrong with her. She tried taping it together that night, but it was ruined. And I never showed her anything ever again."

"You don't want to call her because she would find a way to tear this up too?"

Misti nodded.

"I'm sorry that your mother, the person who should have loved and supported you, tore you down like that."

"It isn't your fault." Misti knew this, but she felt a little weight lift from her shoulders. Her secret was starting to peek through.

When Aunt Mary picked her up from the therapy session, Misti knew her uncle's parents were back at home. Her usually smiling aunt was gripping the steering wheel as if she were trying to choke it.

"Better hurry back." Aunt Mary's voice was not happy. "Your Uncle Bill called. There was an emergency and he's going to be late."

Penny was sitting downstairs looking bored when they got home. Misti could hear a woman talking. Complaining about how cold the house was.

"I'll turn up the heat, Pat," Aunt Mary said carefully, hanging up her coat and gripping Misti's shoulder. Misti smiled at her, trying to encourage her a little.

"Grandma, Grandpa! This is Misti, my cousin."

Misti came into the room. Sitting on the couch were two elderly people, both thin and fragile. The old man stood, extending a shaking hand to Misti. She took it and he squeezed gently before sitting back down and turning back to the TV. He had her uncle's eyes and his big hands. The woman looked Misti up and down. Misti saw no part of her uncle in her. The TV was playing an old black and white Western that Peter, Uncle Bill's father, was watching.

Penny told Misti that they would have to be around a lot while her grandparents visited. Pat was not nice to her mother, but with Penny in the room she kept her remarks to a minimum. If Misti was there, perhaps it would be even less.

Pat was wearing purple pants with light brown orthopedic shoes. Her white top was perfectly pressed and she wore big, gaudy jewelry. She was petite and her hair was short. Misti could tell it was dyed regularly.

"Where were you this afternoon?"

"I told you Grandma, Misti was with a friend." Penny rolled her eyes at Misti. Misti appreciated the cover. Pat did not seem like the type of person who would be okay with therapy. She seemed old school. Bottle it up and don't deal with it.

Aunt Mary rejoined them and prepared dinner with the girls' help. Uncle Bill called and told them to eat without him. He was fixing a blown panel at an apartment complex and wanted to get it done before tomorrow.

"Why on Earth does he care if those people have power or not?" Grandma Pat grumbled. "His mother is only in town a few times a year. He should be home spending time with us."

"He's doing it tonight so he can spend the rest of the week with you," Aunt Mary said through her teeth. Penny and Misti exchanged glances. It would be a long night without Uncle Bill.

After dinner, Aunt Mary turned on an old Western for Grandpa Peter and poured herself a glass of wine. Normally the girls would have gone upstairs. Misti wanted to go up and relax before work tomorrow, but Penny shook her head no and they sat down at the kitchen table to play cards with Grandma Pat.

The game was Rummy and Misti picked it up pretty quickly.

"What time do you need to be at work tomorrow?" Aunt Mary said, after another attempt of conversation with Pat had failed.

"Not until 7:30." Misti picked up a jack, making three. She laid the cards down neatly and discarded a four. Penny made a face before drawing from the deck. Another face. It was a good thing they were not playing poker.

"You got a job?" Pat said, focusing her eyes on Misti.

"I do. I work at a coffee shop."

Grandpa Peter had turned up the TV to an obnoxious level. Aunt Mary's headache was becoming visible.

"You pay rent, then?"

"Uh, no." Misti glanced at her aunt, who had lowered her cards, her face darkening. Penny's eyes widened.

"Why not? You aren't my son's responsibility. Why should he work hard to support a girl he had no part of bringing into this world?"

Misti felt as if she had been slapped in the face while a white rage roared to life in her chest. She was silent, focusing on her cards.

"Mom!" Uncle Bill's arrival had been shielded by the gun fight on the TV. Pat turned and looked at him. "Misti will never have to pay rent in this house. Not that any of this is your business. We want her here. I want her here. She works because she wants to. Not because we asked her to. If she wants to quit and wait until after high school like Penny, that would be fine with me."

Uncle Bill placed his hand on his wife's shoulder.

"I just think..."

"No, Mom. You do not get a say in this. Now, drop it or leave."

Pat looked hard at her cards, her mouth a thin line, but she said no more. Uncle Bill kissed his wife hello and smiled at the girls. Aunt Mary forfeited, getting up to get her husband a plate. Uncle Bill took her place and looked at her hand.

"Did you get the box fixed?" Penny asked.

"Yep. People get to have a nice, warm Christmas now."

Misti knew that they were not among those people.

That night, Misti bunked with Penny, forfeiting her room to the cranky grandparents. She brought her diary, her clothes, and, at the last minute, she grabbed Lily Banks' journal.

They put on a movie on Penny's computer and chatted about school. Misti let Penny drone on and on about Sam and how she hoped that they would move on to more than just talking. Alex had told Misti that Sam was a good guy but painfully shy. Penny would have to make the first move.

"Why don't you just tell him how you feel?" Misti asked. She was on an air mattress on the floor and Penny had convinced her to paint her nails.

"I can't do that! The guy has to make the move first!"

"Who says?"

Penny paused and seemed to be thinking it over. "I would be too scared. What if he doesn't feel the same way?"

"What if he does?"

Penny looked hopeful. "Has Alex said anything?"

"Just that Sam is very shy."

Penny laid down, blowing on her nails. "I don't know if I can do it."

"Just think about it."

They were silent, watching the film for a minutes, letting their nails dry.

"I'm sorry Grandma said those things to you."

"It's not your fault."

"I know, but still…she had no right. You aren't freeloading. You deserve to be treated better."

"Thanks. Not the worst thing anyone has ever said to me."

Penny looked at her waiting for more, but Misti was thinking about her mom's second-to-last boyfriend, who had called her a whore because she pulled a knife on him when he crawled into bed with her one night. Not something you share with your cousin whose main concern in life was whether the boy she liked liked her back.

Misti arrived just as the big rush was starting. She jumped behind the counter, tying on an apron as she clocked in. Abigail looked over at her from the register with a smile.

"Megan called off. So glad you could be here today!"

"You should have called. I could have come in early!"

Abigail shook her head.

"No sense. Rush just started."

The next few hours flew by. Misti could now make almost any fancy coffee without looking up the recipe, while dishing out breakfast pastries and chatting with the regulars. She had grown quite fond of the old man who she had seen sitting outside the first day she drove through town. He came every day and had two coffees, both black with a bear claw, and read the paper. His name was Mr. Allen, but he told Misti to call him Fred.

The walking group they had passed turned out to be led by Alex's stepmom. They would come in on Saturdays and order all lite drinks with coconut milk and no sugar.

Today Misti got to see some new faces: Working people rushing off for half days before the holiday.

Abigail had taken a lunch and Misti was wiping down the machines when the bell rang.

"Hey!"

She smiled, recognizing Alex's voice. "Hey! What can I get you?"

"Caramel frappe please." While she worked he kept talking. "What time do you get off? Do you have time to go up to the city and see a movie?"

"I don't think I can. My uncle's mom is in town and Penny and I have to support my aunt. The lady is a real witch."

Alex looked disappointed. "How much?"

"On me. Payment for all the coffee during school."

He smiled. "Let me know if you can sneak out for a little bit tonight."

"I will."

Alex left and she watched as he jogged across the street and went into the music store.

"How long have you two been dating?" Abigail appeared from the back.

"Dating? We aren't dating! We're just friends."

"Oh...sorry. I figured the way he made you smile, he had to be your boyfriend."

Misti blushed. She knew Alex made her happier. But she also knew that she was allowed to be happy with what they had and it not be anything more.

At the end of the day, just before Misti picked up the last chair, Abigail handed Misti an envelope.

"Thanks!" Misti didn't open it, tucking it into her back pocket.

"Have a great Christmas!" Abigail smiled. "There's a little bonus from the boss in all the checks! Enjoy!"

Aunt Mary picked Misti up. Misti had prepared her a seasonal drink, along with one for everyone else. Grandma Pat took her tea without saying a word and Grandpa Peter looked pleased with his white chocolate mocha.

Misti went upstairs to change and Penny hurried up behind her, following her into her room and slamming the door behind them.

"What is this?" Penny held up Lily's diary.

Sixteen

Sharing

Misti's first instinct was to snatch the diary back. Instead, she kept her hands by her side. "Why were you going through my things?"

"I didn't. I woke up this morning and found this on my night stand, right next to me. I thought you wanted me to read it!"

Misti felt her face drain of color and Penny's eyes widened. "I didn't put it on your night stand. I had it in my bag."

"Misti," Penny set the book down. "Who is Lily Banks? Is that your mom?"

Misti wanted to laugh. Penny didn't even know her own aunt's name. She also missed all the pages where Lily complained about her brother.

"No. I don't know who it is."

"Where did you get it?"

Misti looked at the book again. The color had not returned to her face. "You wouldn't believe me if I told you."

"Try me."

"Girls!" Aunt Mary was at the door. "I need your help with pies."

Misti was grateful for the interruption. Penny's eyes told her that this was not over. Misti changed out of her work clothes, grabbed the diary and put it back with her bag before going down.

Pat was sitting at the island, examining her manicure while the rest of the girls worked on pies. Uncle Bill was sitting on the couch, chatting with his father about someone's season.

Misti had never made a pie before. Over the last month she had learned that her aunt loved to cook and preferred to do everything she could from scratch. They were making a pumpkin pie and an apple pie, but first they were making a crust.

While Misti learned about the importance of grating cold butter into the pie crust mixture, she tried to find a logical way to explain Lily's diary. Nothing she came up with sounded better than the truth.

There was no way around it. She would have to tell Penny about the lock spinning, the girl in the mirror, the arranging of her things for her. And how it all had stopped after finishing the diary.

The pie making took much longer than Misti expected. By the time the pies were in the oven, Grandpa Peter announced he was taking everyone to dinner and they all needed to get dressed in their finest. Penny scurried upstairs and Misti followed, ducking into her own room and grabbing a nice sweater and black skinny jeans.

She had enough time to rinse off and reapply her makeup and let Penny spray her with a bottle of some fruity scent before they were scrambling back down the stairs.

"Don't think I've forgotten," Penny said, heading down the stairs first. "I want to know everything after we go to bed."

Grandma Pat had not really moved in the two hours. She was flipping through one of Aunt Mary's decor magazines. She had not offered to help with the pies, only observing them with a critical eye. She looked over the girls now. Penny had put on an almost identical outfit to

141

Misti.

"You girls plan that?"

Misti and Penny looked at each other and then giggled. Grandma Pat did not look amused.

The pies were taken out of the oven and left to cool in the center of the island on racks. The apple pie looked like a professional had made it and Uncle Bill praised them all, kissing his wife's cheek.

"Perfection," Misti heard him mumble to her so his mother couldn't hear. Aunt Mary smiled for the first time in a few days.

The family went to an Italian restaurant in town and had a pleasant time. The place was packed. Misti saw several of her classmates there, both working and with their families. Most smiled at them. The food was delicious and Misti ate everything put in front of her. She was so full as they walked to the car, she didn't think she could eat again. Penny looked to be in the same boat.

"Good practice stretching out those stomachs for tomorrow!" Uncle Bill laughed.

It was just after 9 when they got home. The adults were discussing what movie they might watch.

"We're going to watch something in my room," Penny announced.

The girls were halfway up the stairs when Uncle Bill roared for them to come back.

They hurried to the kitchen. The pies were destroyed. They had been thrown against the wall and then parts of the filling dragged across the floor.

"Stay here!" Uncle Bill pushed both girls to Aunt Mary. She instictively put an arm around each girl. Uncle Bill grabbed a knife out of the block and headed upstairs.

"Should we go back outside?" Pat asked. The usually calm woman's eyes were panicked. Peter looked like he wanted to follow his son.

"Who would do this?" Aunt Mary said so only Misti and Penny heard. Penny looked just as scared as her grandmother. Misti felt the anxiety that had almost gone away completely sneaking its way back into her chest. She was staring at the wall where the pumpkin pie had been smeared. The words "Lily was here" dripped down. Penny followed her gaze. Her eyes snapped back to Misti.

She would have to be told everything now.

Uncle Bill returned a few minutes later. All windows and doors were locked. There was no one hiding under any beds. The alarm had not gone off and the front door had been locked when the family had returned.

Misti and Penny cleaned up the mess. The first thing they did was wipe the words off the wall. Misti prayed no one but Penny had seen it. Aunt Mary had started to cry, and Uncle Bill ushered her out of the room.

"What's going on!" Penny mouthed at Misti when they were down behind the island wiping up gooey apple pie. Misti shook her head. She honestly didn't know. Uncle Bill returned to help them, saying Aunt Mary would be staying upstairs the rest of the night. Pat was sweeping up the glass from the pie pans.

"Girls."

Misti looked up from where she was scrubbing and Penny stopped wiping the wall.

"Have either of you given a key to anyone?"

They both shook their heads. Misti would never even have thought of doing that. And if Penny did, it would be to Chloe before anyone else.

"The doors were locked. Someone had to get in here. Which means they had to have a key."

"Dad, I swear, I have not given a key to anyone. And Misti either."

"I have not."

Uncle Bill sighed and sat down. "I don't understand."

"Maybe they came in the garage. Is anything else missing?" Grandma Pat spook in a low, calm voice.

"Not that we can tell. Safe is untouched, jewelry is there. You girls should go check your things, but your rooms looked undisturbed. I mean, as undisturbed as teenage rooms can look."

Penny and Misti hurried upstairs. Misti's room was undisturbed. Penny's room looked like it had when they left, except the diary was sitting in the middle of her bed. The girls looked at each other.

"That was not there when we left." Penny glanced over her shoulder, keeping her voice low.

"I have no idea what is going on."

"We need to go finish cleaning up, for Mom. But you need to tell me what is with that diary!"

The clean-up took over an hour. There was pie on almost every surface in the kitchen and some had spread to the living room. Pat managed to get most of the pumpkin pie off the beautiful sofa. Uncle Bill stood on a chair and cleaned off the ceiling. Everyone looked drained by the time it was done. Uncle Bill hugged Penny and shocked Misti when he hugged her, saying in her ear, "If something, or someone, is there, scream. I'll be there."

The girls bid them goodnight and went to Penny's room. The diary had moved again. This time it was sitting on her desk, propped up.

Misti told Penny everything. Penny sat and listened, never interrupting, never pulling a face or rolling her eyes. Instead she kept a neutral face.

"I've had this diary for almost a month. I haven't noticed anything odd." Misti paused. She picked up the diary. "I don't believe in ghosts. Or demons. Or anything supernatural. If I can't see it or touch it, then it isn't real."

"When did you bring the diary home?" Of all the things Penny could have asked, she wanted to know that.

"About four weeks ago. Why?"

"I didn't tell anyone, but I started having weird things happen to me."

Misti waited for more. They heard footsteps in the hall and both quieted. Pat and Peter were making their way to Misti's room for the night. There was a quiet shuffling on the carpet.

"I heard that."

"Me too."

"No, I mean, that was one of the strange things I heard. I would hear someone walk past my room at weird times. It would always wake me up too." Misti thought about the night when she heard her door open and felt fingers on her arm. There had been no one there. She had explained it away as a dream.

"It could have been your parents, or me."

"That's what I thought at first, until one Saturday. You were at work, Dad had gone to the store, and Mom had gone to pick you up. I was in here, the door open, and I heard that noise. I spun around and there was no one there. And all the hairs on my arm stood up. It felt like I was being watched." Penny's brow knotted together. "And I know how my mom and dad sound. I'm even figuring out your sounds. Although you move super quietly." Misti took that as a compliment. "This always sounded different. Like dragging feet."

If Misti hadn't had weird things happen to her too, she probably would not have believed her cousin. She thought about the times, sitting in her room, hearing movement in the hall. She always assumed it was Penny.

"I'm sorry I brought it home. And I'm sorry I kept it home. I didn't know."

"How could you? It's just a diary! Who knew stuff like this could happen because of a book?" Penny leapt up and hurried to her computer. She brought it back to them and started a Google search. For an hour, the girls read together about haunted objects and other supernatural advice. Misti was primarily interested in learning how to make it stop.

"Maybe she just wants us to know her story?" Penny mused. She did another search but they found nothing on Lily Banks. "I know, we can look at old yearbooks. She gives us dates. That will help!"

Misti didn't see how a yearbook would help solve anything, but maybe having a picture of her would give them an idea of where to start. Penny put the computer away.

"It's still pretty shitty of Lily to destroy your mom's pies." Misti stared at the book in her hands. "Not cool, Lily!"

"Yeah. The one thing my mom has against my grandma is the ability to cook."

Misti looked at the time. It was just after midnight. The house was quiet. She wondered what Lily's objection to the Christmas pies were.

"Let's remake them."

"What?" Penny was braiding her hair for bed.

"Let's remake them. For your mom."

Penny hesitated, glancing at her bed for only a moment before nodding. They brought the diary with them, Misti whispering to Lily she was not allowed to destroy anything else in this house. They would figure out her story.

Uncle Bill was still up, the TV turned down so low it was barely audible.

"What are you girls doing?" he asked. Misti saw him quickly slide a gun out of view while she tucked the book behind her back. Uncle Bill still thought something could happen. He was on guard duty.

"We're going to remake the pies." Penny went to the kitchen and started by pulling out her mother's recipe book. Misti tucked the book into her pants while she retrieved the ingredients and the girls set to work, reminding each other of the things Mary had said to them that afternoon. Uncle Bill had turned off the TV and sat watching them at the island, pride glowing in his eyes. The three of them sat up until just after 3. The dishes were redone and put away. The pies were set out to cool.

"Great job, you two. Now, go up and get a little rest. Your mom will probably need extra help with dinner tomorrow."

Seventeen

Christmas

~·ϾꙆꙆϿ·~

Misti woke before Penny. Instead of trying to leave the room, Misti let her sleep. She dug out J from her things.

Dear J,

Things got a little weird yesterday, but telling Penny was actually a relief. I feel she believed me, considering she spent an hour researching haunted objects. Not that any of it was helpful. I still don't understand why Lily, if it was Lily, did that. Was it because Penny read her diary? She obviously wanted her to if she made it visible to her. I did not leave it out for her to find. I'm so glad we remade those pies. I hope they taste okay. It was my first baking attempt without Aunt Mary's supervision. I get why she likes it so much. It is almost soothing, following recipes and creating something so good.

I doubt Uncle Bill slept much last night. Hopefully he can nap today before dinner. I think I hear Pat and Peter up. That means presents will be opened soon. I hope everyone likes what I got them. I hadn't been Christmas shopping before.

First normal Christmas. Well, as normal of a Christmas as you can have when there's a ghost trying to destroy it.

Penny was difficult to wake up, but Misti finally got her up and wrapped in a robe. She was not a girl who handled sleeping less than eight hours well.

They made their way downstairs. When they entered the living area, Aunt Mary wrapped them both in her arms.

"Oh, my beautiful girls. You're too good for me!" She rocked them from side to side.

"Mom!" Penny wiggled away after a minute. "Don't be so dramatic!"

"You remade those pies?" Pat said. The girls nodded. Uncle Bill was up, dark circles under his eyes but a smile on his lips and a large coffee cup in his hands.

"They did." Aunt Mary tried hugging them again but they dodged her, going to the cinnamon rolls on the counter.

"Let's do presents!" Aunt Mary was a different woman from yesterday.

Misti got a new set of drawing pencils, a new sketchbook, a giftcard to the big bookstore, a sweater, shirt, and cash. She did not get anything from Pat and Peter, not that she needed anything. She had not gotten anything for them. This was the most she had ever gotten for Christmas, besides that real Barbie.

She had gotten her uncle a guide to fantasy football and socks for his favorite college team. She caught him reading the book while others were opening their gifts. She got her aunt a famous chef's biography and a new apron. And for Penny, she got her a variety pack of coffees and a book on fashion.

Her gifts went over well. She had gotten them one day after work, when there was time to kill before Aunt Mary came for her.

"You didn't have to," Aunt Mary told her.

Misti just smiled. "Neither did you," she said in her head.

After the wrapping paper had been cleaned up, Misti went back upstairs and put her things down in a small pile next to her temporary bag in Penny's room. She showered and dressed. Penny went in right after she did.

Can I see you sometime today?

It was from Alex.

Sure. This afternoon?

Sounds perfect. I'll text when I'm on my way over.

Misti spent the rest of the morning obsessing over what Alex was coming to see her for. She had gotten him a present. Something silly; she picked it up on impulse. She had also gotten Sarah and Amber something. It was what you did for friends after all. She couldn't get something for them and not for Alex.

Just after 1, Alex said he was on his way. Misti went out front, wrapped in her coat, waiting for him. It had not snowed much this year but it was cold. There were a few people out, some kids riding what she assumed were their new bikes; a man flying his new drone. There was a cozy peace over the neighborhood this morning. The shocking incident of last night was just a memory. Misti wondered if Penny would ever tell her parents. She doubted they would believe her.

Alex arrived about five minutes after she stepped outside. He got out of the car and was carrying a box.

"I just wanted to give you this and say Merry Christmas in person!" he said.

Misti smiled. She knew what she was doing was wrong. She just wanted to keep things as friends. But every time she saw him, let him come over, talked to him, she knew she was leading him on. She suddenly did not want to give him her gift.

"Thanks! Merry Christmas!" She accepted the present. Before she could stop herself, she pulled out her gift from her pocket and handed it to him. He looked surprised that she had gotten him something. Maybe she was reading into this too much. There were two gifts. The first was a drawing that had been framed. It was the one Alex had done without her help. It was a crude attempt at her, Sarah, and Amber. They were laughing at something.

"I had to trace some—well, most of it." He shoved his hands in his pocket.

"It's great! I love it!" She set it aside and opened the little package. It was a necklace, shaped like a compass. Alex's handwriting was underneath.

"I hope this can help you find where you are going."

It was not a cheap necklace, she could tell by the weight. It was silver.

"You don't have to wear it. I just saw it and thought it was something you might like."

Misti did something she had never done before. She stepped forward and hugged him. His body went stiff for just a moment before he hugged her back. Then she felt his arms wrap around her, like a forcefield engulfing around her. She had smelled him every time she got in his car or he plopped next to her. But this time, she really took it in. And she knew that she was lying to herself. She was hiding behind years of hurt to justify being alone. She was using her past as a prediction of the future.

"I love it," she whispered. That compass was pointing her in the right direction. And now she was scared. Misti didn't know how long they stayed like that, but a grunt pulled her back into reality. She looked over her shoulder and blushed when she found Uncle Bill standing there, arms crossed over his chest.

"Alex," he nodded. "Merry Christmas."

"Merry Christmas, sir."

"Dinner is almost ready, Misti."

"Okay. I'll just be a few more minutes."

Uncle Bill nodded before going back inside.

"Better hurry. He probably went to get a weapon," Alex said, pulling out his gift. His cheeks were flushed. From the cold? Misti wondered.

"I don't think you'll be able to use it," Misti said, suddenly seeing the impracticality of her gift.

She had seen a little key chain, with a video game control on it, at the craft store one day a few weeks ago when Mary had dragged her in there after picking her up from work.

"It's great! Alex pretended to play with the remote before pulling out his keys and adding it to the three there. When he was done, he smiled at her. Based on the movies Penny had been making her watch for the past few weeks, this was when he was going to kiss her. She didn't hate the idea.

"Thanks for letting me come see you," he said. They hugged again, not for as long this time.

"Maybe we can do something in a few days?" Misti suggested. Alex nodded and hurried back to his car, waving before ducking into the driver seat and driving away. Misti watched him go, glad that awkward moment was over and also sorry to see him go.

Penny spent an hour Googling the necklace. She and Sam had not exchanged gifts. She said they had agreed that gift giving would complicate what they had. Misti could not argue with her after what she had just experienced with Alex.

"I don't know what he spent, but it's a nice necklace."

The center was a dark stone that sparkled a little and spun around. The lettering and design were etched with precision and care. Misti put it on her neck and it hung at the perfect level. She knew it would be a long time before she took it off.

"Are you still telling me you don't want anything from him?"

They had spent the day with the family playing cards and laughing. Uncle Bill and Aunt Mary had fallen asleep while watching *The Christmas Carol*. The girls had gone to bed and were up chatting. Misti blushed, looking down at her hands.

"I don't know anymore."

"OMG! Really! That's so great!" Penny started jumping up and down on her bed.

"What? Calm down! You'll wake everyone!"

Penny continued jumping but not as high.

Misti struggled to sleep that night. She took stock of her life. She realized that, for the first time, she was what the average person would call in a stable place. She had supportive adults who only wanted the best for her. She had friends and a cousin who she enjoyed hanging out with. And now she had this boy.

"Wonder what Ms. Webb would say?" Misti hoped that her social worker would be happy for her.

Eighteen

The Decision

⸰⸱⸰⸱⸰

Two days after Christmas, Misti waited inside while the rest of the family bid goodbye to Peter and Pat. She had no desire to be a part of that group and knew that she was not wanted. Pat and Peter were spending the next year traveling Europe and they would not be seeing them again for a while. They were considering making a return trip to see Penny, their only grandchild, graduate, but after a few hours of mulling over it and the cost and complications, Aunt Mary had assured them they did not need to bother if it was going to be that big of an issue.

Misti went up to her room and stripped the bedding and washed it. She had texted Alex the day before, hoping they could meet in the coming days and talk. But he and his family had gone on an impromptu skiing trip and would not be back for a few more days.

Nothing odd happened after the pie incident and since Misti had shared what had happened with Penny. Penny had not brought it up again and the girls had discussed other things.

"If I talk to Alex, you have to talk to Sam," Misti said. She was lying on her back, yet another movie playing in the background. Penny looked up from her computer, chewing on her freshly touched-up nails.

"No way!"

"I'm serious. If you really want to be with him, you need to talk to him."

Penny blushed and looked back at her computer skin. "I don't know. He could just be a typical guy. He might not want anything."

"How much time, how many hours, did you waste pining over that asshole Tony?"

Penny groaned. "Don't remind me!"

"Then I don't want to hear it! You need to tell him how you feel. Or move on to find someone who is actually interested in being with you without all these stupid games and no labels."

"Are you really going to talk with Alex?"

"I have to," Misti sighed. "It's only fair."

"At least everyone in the world knows he likes you. You can tell by the way he looks at you."

Misti rolled over and looked at her. "Sam looks at you that way too. You're just too close to see it."

Misti set her things back up in her room, noting that every drawer had been rifled through and her clothes unfolded and moved. Hope you found something interesting, Misti thought to herself. The only thing personal she had was J. And that was always with her.

Penny appeared in her doorway. She looked pale and she was holding a pile of clothes. "I'm going out with Sam tonight. Just the two of us. I'm going to talk to him."

"Good!"

"I have nothing to wear!"

The next hour was devoted to Penny trying on almost every article of clothing she owned. They even raided Misti's closet before she settled on a cute but casual outfit for the adventure. She rattled on constantly, discussing her fears and concerns, accusing Misti of planting this idea and plotting to ruin her life.

"Nothing quite that dramatic."

Misti settled into bed early that night. Penny would be out late and she wanted to give her aunt and uncle some well-deserved alone time with their favorite cooking shows. Plus, she had spent the last week sleeping on an air mattress and had really missed her comfortable bed.

Settling in the fresh sheets, she pulled out J.

Dear J,

Alex texted. He wants to host a small New Year's Eve party at his house. I'll ask Aunt Mary about it but I'm sure if Penny, Sarah, and Amber go, she won't mind. Plus, his father and stepmother will be there. I've made up my mind to speak to Alex and tell him the truth. I know Penny already told him that my mom was crazy and that's why I was here. But I want him to know the truth. I want him to know about that night and why I have kept my distance. I think it is only fair that he should know what he is signing up for. I know that this makes no sense and this is something in those horrible movies that Penny made me watch but I feel like he is the one I am supposed to be with. He just calms me. The second he is around, I feel better. And, despite everything, he hasn't wavered once.

I'm also glad that the weird things around the house have stopped. I don't know what Lily was after or why she wanted to ruin Christmas. It seems silly.

I hope things go well for Penny.

Misti slept through the night and woke early the next morning for her shift. Aunt Mary was humming to herself on the trip to the coffee shop. She could not have made it more obvious about her happiness that her inlaws were gone again. Misti could not blame her. Pat was full of backhanded compliments that she only said when her son was not around.

Work went painfully slowly. The weather was awful and no one was out and about. Abigail left Misti to clean the store while she ran errands, taking a deposit to the bank, going to get a refill of supplies from the store. Misti suspected that she was seeing one of the clerks at the bank; she was so happy when she returned.

"Any New Year's Resolutions?"

Misti shook her head.

"I'm going to try and run every day. Hard when you work such odd hours. But I think it might be good for me to leave the shop and go out. Get rid of some stress. Maybe by spring I'll be able to run in a marathon!"

"I just want to graduate high school."

"Yeah, senior year is hard. Not because the classes were hard but the getting up and going. I mean, by that point, nothing new was ever happening. No new drama, nothing."

Misti wished she could say that there was no "new" for her. But everything this year had been new. A new stable home, a new school, friends, and now a possible boyfriend. By May, she had no idea what to expect. She rubbed her compass necklace between her fingers and thought for a few moments.

"I think it will be okay."

Abigail nodded in agreement, flipping through the running magazine she had come back with.

Penny picked up Misti after work. She was bouncing in her seat.

"I did it!" she shouted the second the door opened.

Misti slipped into the passenger seat.

"I did what you said. I said, 'Sam, we've been doing this talking thing for like ever now and I want to know if you want more or if you just want to be friends'." She backed out of the spot. "There was like a super-long silence that I can't even begin to describe. He just stared at me, a french fry hanging out of his mouth. I was mortified. But then he said the sweetest thing. 'I thought we were dating!'" Penny beamed. "Can you believe it! I have an actual boyfriend."

Misti offered her congratulations. She knew it would work out well for her. Penny rambled the entire way home, telling Misti how wonderful their conversation was now because there was no pressure. They knew that the other liked them and they could just be together. It was the greatest date.

"I'm so glad you pushed me." Penny put the parking brake on the car and turned off the ignition. "I almost called Chloe. Just to rub her face in it. You heard about what happened, right?"

Misti shook her head.

"Tony totally dumped her. At one of the parties, she caught him making out with some sophomore. And he said, 'We aren't a thing, babe.'" Penny did not smile. She rubbed her thumb on her steering wheel.

"You should call her," Misti said. "But ask her if she's okay. Don't be the bitch."

Penny smiled a little.

"Even if she deserves it."

"Oh! Sam said Alex is having a New Year's Eve party and invited me. Are you going?"

"I haven't asked yet but I would like to."

"Mom won't be the problem. It will be Dad."

"I'm pretty sure Alex's parents will be there. And there won't be any alcohol."

158

"Yeah. We'll team up on him tonight. Make him crack!" Penny did not look convinced of her plan.

As they suspected, Aunt Mary was on board with the girls going to the party. Uncle Bill was a little more hesitant.

"It's just a small group of friends, Dad. The same ones we've been doing things with for months."

"And they'll be together. It isn't like they want to go to two separate parties."

"We promise to keep each other safe." Penny looked at Misti for help. Uncle Bill also looked at her. She offered him her best smile and a nod. She would keep them safe.

"Will the parents be there?"

"Yes!" Penny said. "Please, Dad?"

Uncle Bill sighed.

Nineteen

New Year's Eve

⚶⚶⚶

Misti let Penny pick out her outfit: a pair of dark skinny jeans with a couple of fashion-savvy rips, a white shirt that Penny tied in a small knot at her hip, and her jean jacket. The girls curled their hair and put on more makeup than usual. Misti felt nothing like herself. By the time she was at the party, she had untied the T-shirt and wanted to wipe off all the extra makeup.

She and Penny arrived at the same time as Amber, who was also glammed up, making Misti feel like she fit in a little more. She was nervous. Beyond nervous. She didn't know if she and Alex would ever be alone long enough for her to tell him of her change of heart. She clutched her necklace on the ride over, reminding herself that this leap was going to be worth it.

"Hey!" Amber ran over and gave Misti a hug. "It feels like it's been forever! Aren't you excited for tonight?"

Misti nodded while Amber and Penny complimented each other's outfits.

There were several more cars than Misti was expecting. She

recognized Sam's and Sarah's. She didn't know anyone else's. They knocked on the door and Alex opened it a few minutes later. Music and light spilled out onto them along with the smell of pizza. Alex smiled at them and Misti's heart jumped up into the back of her mouth. She forced a smile and she watched as his eyes landed on the necklace.

"Thanks for coming! Party is downstairs."

The girls followed their host down the stairs, waving hello to Alex's father, who was leaning back on the couch, head cradled in his hands, eyes fixed on the biggest TV Misti had seen outside a store. Alex's stepmother was nowhere to be seen.

Downstairs there was already a small crowd. Misti waved to Sarah, who was standing with Emily and Sam. Misti recognized a few other kids from school. There was a table set up with pizza, soda, candy, cake, and cookies. Sam broke away from the group when he saw Penny, moving towards her as if under a spell. Misti felt awkward when they kissed, widening her eyes in shock at Amber, who stared open-mouthed before pushing her friend away towards Sarah and Emily.

"Happy New Year!" Emily chirped. She honked the kazoo in her hand and giggled.

"Happy New Year!" Misti had grown to like Emily, especially when she learned that she was not a rival for Alex's affection.

Misti poured herself a root beer and took a slice of pepperoni pizza before sitting on the couch. Alex had dashed back upstairs, bringing more people down. She looked up and found him chatting with friends.

The party had a slow start. Finally, Emily busted out a game called Cards Against Humanity and a large group of people gathered to play.

For over an hour, the group giggled and blushed and howled and whistled as cards were laid out. By the end, Amber won with seven cards. Misti was helping collect the cards when Alex knelt down next to her.

"Glad you like your necklace."

"I love it. You know me so well."

He smiled and looked around. "Think everyone is having fun?"

"Yeah! Better than sitting at home with our families, watching some crap on TV."

There was a long pause.

"Can I talk to you about something?" She felt the words come out of her mouth and knew that this was a now or never moment.

"Sure!" They stood up and started to head out of the room when the doorbell rang. Alex frowned, glancing around. "Be right back!"

Misti let out the breath she didn't realize she was holding as he took the stairs two at a time. She glanced over at Penny, who tilted her head. Misti shrugged back. She moved away from the card game, biting her thumb the way her cousin did. She took her hand away from her mouth and replayed what she was going to say to him again.

"Alex, I know I said that I didn't want to be anything more than friends. But, I think I was lying to myself and I realize now that it wasn't fair to you. If you want, I would like to maybe be more."

She sighed. How cheesy. And at no point did she mention her mother.

Alex came back down the stairs with a tall, beautiful girl with long, blonde hair and blue eyes. She wore a pretty pink dress with knee-high tan boots. She looked like a model straight off of Instagram.

"Hailey! You made it!" Emily dashed forward and threw her arms around the girl.

"Everyone, this is my little cousin Hailey. She's in town visiting."

Emily threw out names so rapidly there was no way the new arrival would remember any of them. But she smiled through it, making eye contact with all of them.

Music suddenly started up and Amber was grabbing Misti, pulling her to the middle of the group to dance. Misti tried to concentrate on her friend but her eyes kept going back to look at Alex, who was talking to Hailey. They were laughing and then she was touching his arm.

Misti broke away from the dancing after attempting something called the Cupid Shuffle. She was walking towards Alex, hoping they could slip away, when she watched Hailey pull him on the floor without much resistance. He was giving her a sloppy grin. As they moved past Misti, she knew he didn't even see her.

Misti turned and watched as Hailey flirted and danced against Alex and watched Alex not mind.

"Who the hell is that girl?" Penny whispered next to her.

"Emily's cousin," Misti murmured. Her heart had dropped from her throat down to her belly button. She moved to the table, picking up a cupcake and taking her time to unwrap it.

"It's like they never stopped dating!" Emily said to Sarah. Misti looked at Sarah, who frowned.

"They know each other?"

"Oh, yeah. They dated for, like, two years." Emily chewed a cookie. "She is being scouted to be a model."

Misti frowned. Alex had never mentioned this to her before.

Sarah also seemed confused. "She seems a little…not his type," she said.

"That's why she's perfect for him! He needs someone to be in charge of him. He's too nice."

A new song came on and Emily squealed in delight, grabbed Sarah's hand and pulled her to the floor. Misti looked at the clock. It was a little after 10.

"Should we go home?" Penny asked. Sam was hanging behind them.

"No, it's okay." Misti smiled. She took her cousin's hand and hooked arms with Sam. "Let's go dance!"

Misti couldn't help but watch as Alex and Hailey slowly moved closer and closer on the dance floor until she was wrapped around him.

At least Misti saw what Alex was really like before she invested any real time into him. Now she knew they were better off as friends.

Just before midnight, Misti let Amber pour her some sparkling grape juice. They were chatting about going to a movie next week when Alex came over to them.

"Could you maybe stop dry humping the new girl in front of everyone, please?" Amber snapped at him. Alex looked dazed. He had a slight grin on his face until his eyes moved to Misti. The smile faded.

"You wanted to talk to me?"

"Another time," Misti shrugged.

"Are you sure?"

"Yeah. I wouldn't want to distract you. You seem to be having a good time."

The words seemed to sting him. Good. He grabbed two cups and filled the drinks before turning away from them.

"Men are assholes," Amber mumbled, eating a cookie. Misti didn't argue.

At midnight, Penny kissed Sam, Emily kissed Sarah, and Hailey grabbed Alex and kissed him. Amber and Misti cheered their cookies.

"I'm so sorry, Misti," Penny said as they pulled out of his driveway. They had to be home by 1. Sam had walked them to their car while the others hung back. Alex stood on the porch with Hailey. Misti looked back to see him watching her. She had gotten into the car without smiling.

It was her fault. She had told Alex she wanted to be friends. And she had treated him like a friend. She was the one who didn't want anything more. This was her fault.

He sure did have a way of making it hurt.

They arrived home to Uncle Bill heading up to bed.

"Was it everything you hoped it would be?" he asked them.

"Could have been better," Penny said. "Wasn't as bad as sitting with my parents while they watched old movies."

"We're cool! We could have watched a new movie."

Penny sighed loudly at her father and he told them both good night before disappearing into his room.

Misti managed to make casual conversation as the girls readied for bed. Penny was going to have Sam over to dinner to meet her parents the next week and she was going to go over to his as well.

"Again, Misti, I'm sorry. Alex is the last person I thought would act like that. Especially with a girl he had just met."

"They dated before. Emily told me."

Penny frowned.

"It's okay. At least it happened before I said anything. Would have been a really awkward night if I had!" Misti smiled but Penny did not return it. "Now when I say we're just friends, people will know it's true." Penny sighed. "I'm beat. I'll see you in the morning."

Misti went to her room, closing the door quietly. She went to her dresser and took her the compass necklace. She held it in her hand, staring at the picture he had drawn. Setting the necklace down in she climbed into bed and put the blankets over her head. She did not let herself cry.

The next day, Misti did her best to act as if nothing happened. She replied to Amber and Sarah that she was fine. She and Alex were just friends. After last night, could they finally see that? Penny kept looking at her over breakfast and lunch with sad eyes but said nothing. Misti wished she was working but the coffee shop was not open for the holiday. Although she put on a brave face for the world, Misti felt an ache in her gut. She had let herself believe for a moment that Alex would be something special and that he would be worth the work and the pain and the fuss. She scolded herself for letting her guard down and allowing him into her world.

Like she told Penny last night, she was glad that it had happened before she shared all those things she wanted to share. It would have been worse if she had shared her deepest secrets with him.

At work the next day, she managed to forget about Alex and focus on the tasks at hand. The cafe was busy with people going back to work. Misti enjoyed working the day shift during the week. They had a little more traffic of people heading to work, which meant a few more tips. On that day, she was working with the other manager. She was not as chatty as Abigail and left her in the front alone once the rush was over. Misti went back to the storage area once and found her on her phone, listening to music.

Misti was restocking the pastries when the bell dinged. Her stomach dropped when she looked up. It was Alex. He was alone. He came up to the counter, dragging his feet, hands shoved into his pockets. He wore his usual black T-shirt and jean jacket. Misti hated that she noticed the tension in his face.

"Hi. What can I get you?"

"I'm okay. I just wanted to talk." Alex's usual confident voice was faint.

"About what?"

Alex sighed and looked over his shoulder. She knew why he was there. But she wanted him to say it out loud. He needed to feel a little bad.

"About the party, and Hailey."

"Your girlfriend."

"She's not my girlfriend."

"Sure did look like a girlfriend when you were kissing her at midnight."

"She was my ex-girlfriend."

"Was. What is she now? Some girl you screw around with once in a while?" Misti felt how harsh the words were when they were leaving her mouth. She had her own forcefield up now. She didn't need his. Alex's eyes narrowed. "I don't think you have any right to be mad."

Misti smiled. And she knew that wasn't what he was expecting. "I'm not mad. I'm confused as to why you're here explaining yourself to me if you aren't worried about how I feel."

There was a pause. The door chimed and two older ladies came in carrying bags from the craft store across the street. Misti excused herself from Alex and helped them, making small talk and looking at their projects until Alex took the hint and left.

He was right. She had made it clear that she didn't want anything from him.

But he had also promised that he would stick around a while and wait for her.

He didn't last three months. If he couldn't wait it out long enough to let her get settled into this new life and get comfortable then what other promises would he take away in three months?

Good riddance.

Twenty

Refocusing

The weekend before school was back, Amber invited Misti to drive up to the city to go shopping. Sarah joined them and Misti was excited for a girls' weekend. She had some money to spend and had her eyes on some boots.

Amber and Sarah made small talk and avoided the Alex conversation until halfway to the city.

"I still can't believe he's back with her!" Sarah blurted out. Amber glanced at Misti, who was in the front seat. Misti sipped her coffee. She had treated her friends to her discount at the store for their road trip beverage.

"It was your girlfriend who brought her to the party," Amber pointed out.

"I know! It's a good thing she's so cute!"

They fell silent. Misti hoped that was the end of the conversation and was thinking of a new subject to get them off of this one.

"Misti, I know you say you and Alex are just friends, but…" Amber paused, adjusting her hands on the wheel. "I saw the way you interacted.

There was something more there, wasn't there?"

"It could have been. But now there probably won't be." Misti gave in a little. "Alex is a big boy. If he can't see that Hailey isn't actually interested in him then that's his problem. And maybe she really is. You don't know."

Misti found the boots she wanted on clearance, leaving her with enough money to buy a new diary. Her old one was full. Amber and Sarah had their parents' credit cards. Misti raised her eyebrows when she saw Amber's bill at the store.

"Shopping is my therapy. And my parents try to buy my love with money. It works out all around." She grinned, but Misti saw in her eyes that it wasn't working out all around.

The girls discussed their classes for the next semester. Misti was allowed to take an extended absence in the afternoon to go to work; she would only be at school for three hours a day. Before the holiday, she was regretting that decision. Now she was glad she had talked her aunt and uncle into letting her do it. She was also starting to consider the community college in the city. She didn't know what she wanted to do yet but she figured that might be a good way to start. Plus, her uncle had dropped hints that it might be good for her to get something figured out.

Misti was sitting in the backseat on the way home when her phone dinged. Expecting it to be Aunt Mary checking in on her, she opened her phone without checking first. Instead, it was Alex.

"Shit," Misti grumbled too loud.

"What is it?"

To her surprise, Misti passed the phone forward and Sarah read the message out loud.

"Can we meet tonight? I just want to talk?"

Misti told them about him coming to the coffee shop and wanting to talk then.

"Oh, how nice of him to bother you while you're working and can't get emotional!" Amber rolled her eyes.

"I don't want to talk to him. I don't want an explanation. We all saw him with her."

"Maybe you should do it. Just to have closure," Sarah offered.

Closure. An ending to something. Not really her family style. She was much more a duck-out-and-leave-without-a-note sort of person. But she was trying to be different here. Being different had been nice.

"Fine."

Amber dropped Misti at home just before 5. Both Amber and Sarah demanded that Misti text them as soon as she could after the conversation with Alex.

Aunt Mary and Uncle Bill were out for the night and Penny was over at Sam's. For the first time in the five months that she lived there, Misti was alone in the house. Aunt Mary had left her homemade mac and cheese for dinner that she heated up with delight. Her aunt had left her a note:

Hope shopping with the girls was fun! We might be late! Enjoy supper! Love Aunt Mary.

Misti ate on the couch, which was strictly prohibited except during pizza night and important sports games. She turned on Netflix and started another episode on *Gossip Girl*, something Penny had gotten her hooked on.

She was on her second episode when she heard footsteps coming down the hall from the foyer. She turned, expecting Penny by the lightness of the steps. The steps stopped. No one was there.

"Penny?" Misti got up, quickly picking up her bowl, which was not set on a coaster, and moved to look down the hall. The door was firmly shut. Misti set the bowl on the counter and walked towards the stairs. She must have misheard; Penny must have gone upstairs. If she was home this early, dinner with Sam's family had not gone well. She walked up the stairs, preparing for an upset Penny. Her door was shut.

"Penny?" Misti tapped lightly on the door. No response. Pressing her ear to the door, Misti strained to hear something. But there was nothing. Carefully, knowing this was against the unspoken rules the girls had established about their rooms, she opened the door and peeked inside. The bed was made and the lights were off. Penny's computer was on her desk and a pile of rejected outfits lay on the bed.

Misti felt a tingle race up her spine. She snapped the door shut and stomped down the stairs, filling the now too quiet house with as much noise as possible. She turned *Gossip Girl* up and laid down on the couch, pulling a blanket over her. She felt safer with her head hidden from view.

"You're just imagining things. This is your first time alone here. You aren't used to the sounds of this big empty place. Watch your show!" she told herself.

The footsteps came again. This time directly behind the couch. Misti ignored them. The steps went by again, stopping at her feet. She kept her eyes fixed on the screen, pretending to be fully absorbed by the beautiful girls. Shattering glass caused her to bolt up. There was no one there, as she knew there wouldn't be. But her empty bowl of mac and cheese lay shattered on the kitchen floor, several feet from the counter.

"What do you want, Lily?" she asked. There was no response. Of course there wouldn't be a response. Why would there be?

Misti swept up the shattered piece of the bowl and scrubbed the cheese that had exploded all over the floor. She dumped the bowl and jumped when the doorbell rang.

She went to the door and opened it, not surprised to find Alex there.

"You're early," she said. She pulled on her shoes and tugged on her coat. She had told her aunt and uncle she would be going back out for a few hours after dinner. She did not specify with whom. She walked down the steps and sat in his car.

Alex drove them to the drive-in. It was empty except for a mom and her son, both having milkshakes.

"Do you want something?"

The chill that had consumed her body while she cleaned the shattered bowl had not left her, but she ordered a small milkshake. Ice cream was needed for a pre-dating breakup.

"Thanks for coming out tonight," he said after they ordered.

"It seemed important to you."

"I just really want you to understand that Hailey and I were not a thing that night."

"Are you a thing now?"

Alex paused, his green eyes scanning her face for any sign of emotion. But Misti had learned a long time ago that showing emotion was a weakness. "I don't know. It's complicated."

"Not really. You're either seeing her or not."

"We're just talking again. We used to date."

"I know."

He looked away, his face flushing.

"Look, Alex. As far as I know, you told me you liked me, and I told you I needed time. If you didn't want to wait for me, that's okay."

"I did want to wait for you." He leaned back against his seat, his fingers strumming the wheel. Misti sat, her hands tucked under her thighs, casually watching him. Her eyes went to his keys still in the ignition. The little key chain she had gotten him dangled there. The necklace was still on the dresser. She had not put it back on since the New Year's Eve party.

"It's okay, Alex." She heard her voice break a little. "You don't owe

172

me anything. I wasn't ready when you were. We just missed each other's window."

It was her turn to face away, gathering her emotions. She felt his eyes land on her.

"I just...Hailey and I dated for almost two years. And we broke up for a really stupid reason. I feel like I owe her."

There was a long pause. The carhop brought them their milkshakes and Misti took several gulps, suppressing tears with chocolate creaminess.

"What was the stupid reason?" she spoke quietly, wondering he could even hear her. She just wanted to break the silence.

"You don't want to know."

"Wouldn't ask if I didn't want to know." Misti knew her voice sounded irritated.

"She wanted me to hang out with Sam less. I wanted her to stop wearing so much makeup."

Misti didn't say anything.

"We were young."

"Wasn't it just last year?"

"Yeah. But a lot has changed."

"Like hanging out with Sam?"

There was another long silence.

"How much longer would that window have been closed? I mean yours, not mine?"

Misti was not prepared for that question. She continued to look out the window, watching an older couple, sharing a sundae. She could tell him the truth and see what happened. Would it matter that she was ready that night to tell him, to give them a chance? If she had spoken to him, pulled him aside the second she got there and told him that she was falling for him, that she was ready to be with him, would that midnight kiss have been hers? Would they be sharing a treat now, instead of facing away from each other?

"I don't know."

Alex drove her back to her house and as they got closer, fear of the house and regret over not telling him consumed her. She blinked back tears. She didn't want to go into the house and be alone with Lily. But she could not stay in the car and let Alex see her cry.

"See you Monday!" She leapt out of the car before it came to a full stop, hurrying up the stairs.

"Misti!" he called. Her hands were shaking and her eyes were blurring. She managed to get the key in the door and tumbled inside, slamming the door behind her. She slid down, tucking her knees to her chest, and let the tears fall silently. She heard Alex outside the door but he did not knock. He waited only a few moments before she heard his steps retreat and his car drive away.

Ten minutes later, Misti pushed herself up and dragged herself upstairs. A long, hot shower would help her. She stood, letting the water cascade over her, washing away all the tears. She was done crying over him. This was a good thing. She didn't need to love him. Because in the end, it would hurt more when he left. And he would leave. For his music, for another girl. He would go.

She did not know how long she was in the shower but the steam had filled the room. She stepped out onto the rug, and her eyes settled on the mirror.

HELP ME

Twenty-One

Lily makes Contact

Misti wasn't sure how long she stood dripping water on the bathroom floor. Her heart was thundering in her chest and she was afraid to look around the room. The door was firmly shut and locked, a habit she had not broken from her days with her mother. Gathering courage, she stepped forward slowly and picked up her phone. Her hand was trembling slightly. She gripped the towel against her chest and opened the camera, snapping, one, two, three pictures of the writing. She lowered the phone. The steam was dissipating and her fear jumped to a new level. Instincts told her if she stayed there and the mirror began to appear, she would see the same girl from her locker, standing behind her, reaching for her. Stepping to the door, she unlocked it and hurried down the hall to her room, firmly shutting the door behind her. Sitting on the bed, still wet, she forced herself to take calming deep breaths. This was getting weird.

Footsteps outside her door made the hammering in her chest increased. The steps were slow and steady. They stopped outside her room.

"Misti?" Aunt Mary's voice called through the door. Relief flooded her body.

"Yes! Hi! Just got out of the shower, I'll be down in a minute!" she spoke so quickly, she was sure Aunt Mary suspected something.

"No rush, dear, just checking on you." The footsteps returned down the hall. Misti dressed quickly in sweats and a shirt before hurrying down to join her guardians.

Uncle Bill was on the couch, TV already on, beer in hand.

"How was game night?" Misti asked.

"Oh, typical. Fun at first but by the end of it we just wanted to be home with our kids, watching our dumb shows."

Aunt Mary smiled at her. The negativity Misti had felt before their return was floating away.

"Anything exciting happened while we were gone?" Uncle Bill asked.

"Not really." Misti knew if she told them, they would not believe her anyway. They might suspect her of being like her mother. That wouldn't be good. Misti did apologize for breaking the bowl.

"I thought it was on the counter but I misjudged, I guess."

"It's okay. Accidents happen. As long as you weren't hurt."

Misti settled into the couch and watched the shows with her aunt and uncle. She knew if she left them and went back upstairs, she would find a different kind of company waiting for her.

Penny arrived about an hour later, glowing. Her visit had been a success. Sam's parents had loved her.

"What's not to love?" Aunt Mary responded. Penny didn't even roll her eyes.

"When does he come here?" Uncle Bill asked.

"Soon, Dad," she told him. Penny nodded her head towards upstairs and Misti rose.

"Goodnight, girls! Sweet dreams!"

They clambered up the stairs, dashing to Penny's room and shutting the door quickly.

"Sam's family is so nice! His mom is like this real hippie chick and his dad is all rock 'n' roll. They're so laid back and supportive of their son. It's amazing!" Penny plopped onto the bed with a happy sigh. She tilted her head at Misti. "What?"

Misti told her about the footsteps, the bowl, the writing on the mirror. She showed her the pictures. Penny listened to it all, staring at the pictures.

"I know what you are thinking, that I wrote that. But I swear, I did not."

"I know you didn't. She was answering your question. She wants our help."

A week had gone by and the girls had returned to school. Misti was glad to be back in the routine and grateful that she was no longer in Art. Amber told her that Alex sat and pouted through class, not working on their assignment. Misti didn't really care.

Despite the haunting being terrifying, Misti was happy for the distraction. First thing on Monday, she returned the journal to the locker and, under her breath, told Lily she needed to stay there and not come home with her any more. She also let her know that she and Penny were going to investigate and figure out what happened to her.

Penny said the first thing she was going to do was get a hold of the yearbooks that Lily would have been in. She wanted to see if it was the girl that they had been dreaming about. When Misti came home from work on Monday, Penny reported that all yearbooks older than ten years were locked away. And she had no reason to ask for permission to see them.

"Mr. Miller is super strict about letting anyone into the storage room. I'm not sure why."

Misti wasn't too disappointed. She wasn't sure what a yearbook would tell them besides give them a picture of the dead girl.

On Wednesday, Misti came out of work to find Penny bouncing on her toes waiting for her. "I know how we can get it!"

The plan was pretty simple, according to Penny. On Thursday night, Penny loaned Misti another school shirt and the girls set out for the home basketball game. Penny had signed up to cover it.

"Look at my responsible editor!" Mr. Miller called when he saw them coming down the hall. Penny smiled widely. "Make sure you get some good shots!" Mr. Miller let Misti in without having her pay.

The girls spent the first quarter pretending to be there on yearbook assignment. Misti knew nothing about basketball and watched the crowd instead. She saw Amber sitting with the crowd and waved. The crowd was similar to the football group. The same boys with painted chests were present. Their chests were painted again but they had added crazy hair and aviator sunglasses. The cheerleaders had dwindled in population due to an outbreak of mono and the usual lively bunch were hanging back, only offering cheers every twenty minutes or so.

"Okay, I have enough. Let's go!"

They stood and Penny led the way to Mr. Miller, who was standing in the doorway, watching the game.

"What's up?"

"The camera's dead! Can I go get another charger?"

Mr. Miller looked over at the game, which was very close in score and then back at Penny.

"You don't have to come. I promise not to burn down the school."

Mr. Miller grinned and pulled out his keys. Penny snatched them before he could change his mind and the girls walked down the hall.

"We need to hurry. He can't suspect anything!"

They took the stairs up to the yearbook room two at a time. The empty hallways of the school made Misti's skin crawl. The usual bustle and noise was gone and the only sound was their steps down the tile hallway.

Penny found the correct key on the jumble of a ring and opened the door. The door slammed behind them, causing them to jump and then giggle at each other.

Penny led the way to the back of the room. She found a different key and opened the lock on the door. They stepped inside and had to use their phones' lights to find the overhanging pull light.

It was a large closet, with shelves containing books, dust, an old computer monitor, and the reason no one was allowed back in the room. A a stash of booze, cigarettes and chewing tobacco. Penny sighed.

"I always heard the rumors about a teacher selling that stuff. I figured it was Mr. Hill doing it."

The girls worked quickly. Despite the look of it, the room was organized and Penny found the old yearbooks. She found the one from 2000 and they moved out of the room, turning off the light as they went. Penny slipped the yearbook into her camera bag and they hurried back down the steps.

"Took you long enough. Was about to come looking for you!" Misti couldn't look at the man. She focused on the game, as if she knew what was going on.

"Sorry! We had to pee!" Penny lied so well.

"TMI, McGrath!" He looked from girl to girl. Penny was blushing as they walked away.

"It will be hard to look at him on Monday!" Misti caught herself giggling.

Back at home, the girls retreated to Penny's room. They pulled out the yearbook and started looking through it.

"That's the girl from my dream!" Misti pointed at Lily. She was standing in the drama club photo, holding a notebook to her chest. She was pretty, with blonde hair in a high ponytail. Next to her was a shorter, pudgy girl. Shannon.

At the end of the yearbook, the girls found a memorial page.

For Lily: Taken too soon.

"I guess it's true!" Penny looked shocked. There was a different picture of Lily. It must have been one of her senior pictures. She looked happy and innocent. Misti wondered if this picture was taken before she met H.

Misti flipped to the teacher section. Penny gave her a puzzled look. There were not many teachers and it did not take Misti long to figure out who "H" was.

"Henry Wilks." She pointed to the teacher. He was young in the picture, probably only in his mid-twenties. Penny furrowed her brow. Misti flipped back to the picture from the Drama Club. Standing next to Lily was Mr. Wilks. Or H. Of course. Lily had mentioned that she was the stage manager and able to speak to him whenever without suspicion because of it.

"You aren't going to believe this." Penny stood up and moved to her desk, opening her computer. She typed Henry Wilks' name into the search bar.

Henry Wilks had not changed much in the twenty years since the picture Misti was holding was taken. He had more wrinkles on his face and his hair was thinner. But it was definitely him. Henry Wilks was the superintendent of the school district now.

"That's crazy!"

"Mom and Dad are friends with him. He's been here for BBQs." The girls gathered snacks before settling into their detective session for the night.

"I think we need a list of suspects." Misti threw a handful of potato chips in her mouth.

"Obviously Henry is at the top of the list." Penny flipped open a notebook and wrote down his name.

"And Brian." Misti wiped the salt from her fingers and picked up the yearbook. She started flipping through the pictures. She found Brian's face and it sucked the air out of her for a moment. It was like looking at Alex.

"Brian Turner." She held out the yearbook to Penny. Her eyes widened and she locked eyes with Misti. He was Alex's father.

"Why would Brian kill Lily?" Penny asked. They could not determine any more suspects. They only had the journal to go off of.

"He figured out that Lily was going to set him up? Do you think Sam would like it if you did that to him?"

"Fair point."

"And Henry could have found out that he was the father and needed to silence her. She was a minor and it could cost him his career. Maybe even send him to jail."

"So both our suspects have two really good motives." Penny plopped back. "Awesome."

They sat in silence. A twenty-year-old cold case was hard to solve for professionals. How were they supposed to do it with nothing but a journal and a ghost who kept throwing temper tantrums?

"Does this town have a library?"

Twenty-Two

Digging up Dirt

At the library the next day, the girls trailed behind a rail-thin woman wearing mothball-smelling clothes. She whispered instructions on how to use the reel and the girls began looking back at the newspapers for a "school" project. The yearbook had given them the date of Lily's death and it did not take long for the girls to find what they were looking for.

"Lily Banks was found bludgeoned to death in the parking lot of the high school by a group of her classmates. Police were called to the site immediately. Witnesses reported seeing Lily and her boyfriend, Brian Turner, leaving the dance about twenty minutes before. Brian was found sitting out on the football field. He reports that the two had gotten into a fight by his car and he left her there. The school has canceled classes on Monday as the police continue to search for evidence. The murder weapon was found next to the victim. Anyone with information is asked to come forward."

"That's horrible!" Penny whispered.

"What's horrible?" The girls snapped their heads and found Amber standing in the doorway, cradling two books. "What are you guys doing?"

Misti and Penny looked at each other. Amber was one of the smartest girls in the school. She might not be the worst person in the world to talk to.

"Shut the door," Misti invited her in.

Amber listened to their story, showing very little emotion as they did. She read the news article before saying, "I thought you said nothing weird was going on with your locker?"

Misti wanted to laugh. "I didn't want you all to think I was crazy."

"But she's not crazy because it happened in our home. My parents can even tell you about that night. Well, they don't know about the ghost thing, but they saw the pies."

"And we have evidence that something happened. Just like everyone said."

Penny and Misti held their breath, waiting for Amber to say something.

"We need to talk to Sarah."

Sarah met the girls at the drive-in. She didn't need much convincing to come. She slid into the backseat of Penny's Camry and accepted the milkshake that had arrived just before she got there.

"What's up, guys? Why do you all look so weird?"

Misti and Penny told the story again. Sarah leaned forward at the mention of the ghost, her eyes coming alive. Misti showed them both the picture from the bathroom.

"That's crazy! Misti, you should have told me sooner! I love ghost stuff!" Sarah zoomed in on the picture.

"That's why we called you. It seems this ghost needs help and you're the only person I know who even knows about ghosts."

"There isn't any one proven way to talk to ghosts." Sarah handed the phone back to Misti. "But there are a few things we can try."

"If we can figure this out, do you think it will help Lily find peace?"

"Maybe. Some do; some never go away. But it seems like she wants you to do something." Sarah leaned back, pulling out her own phone. "Is she attached to the locker?"

"No, I think she's attached to the diary."

"Do you have it still?"

Misti shook her head. "It's at school. With the weird things happening at home, we decided it would be best to keep it there."

"That's okay. It will give us time to prepare."

The next Monday, Sarah was waiting for Misti at her locker. Misti was glad someone was waiting there. Ever since their pre-dating breakup, she had not seen or spoken to Alex.

Misti opened the locker and took out the diary. "Lily, this is Sarah. She's going to help us. But to do that, she needs to borrow this for a while. I hope that's okay."

"Have you always talked to her like that?"

"Yea." Misti took out her things for English and the girls walked to class together. "She was pretty nice at first. She would organize my stuff for class or for the end of the day. She only scared me when she showed herself in the mirror. And when she did that stuff at home."

"She was just desperate. You're probably the first person to acknowledge her in twenty years."

Alex appeared around the corner, carrying his usual morning coffee, headphones in, looking at his phone. Misti ducked into the next hall, dragging Sarah with her.

"Well, that answers my question about how you two are doing." Sarah dramatically adjusted her clothes.

"Sorry. I haven't talked to him since the drive-in."

"I don't blame you. He's a total asshat. Emily and I have banned the topic as it resulted in a near breakup-worthy fight."

"I'm sorry." Misti blushed in shame.

"Don't be. Hailey is her cousin so she defends her. But you're one of my best friends so of course I'm going to defend you."

Misti smiled. At least something good had come out of all of this. She had a best friend.

That Friday, Sam came over to dinner. Misti came home from work to find Penny in a near-frantic state. She couldn't decide what to wear or what to do with her hair.

"It's not like he's here to meet you for the first time. It's his job to look good for your parents. And he's a nice guy. He'll do fine. You know—unless Uncle Bill kills him and chops him up in the wood chipper."

"You're not funny, Misti."

Uncle Bill had been searching online for wood chippers all week, making sure to make comments about them whenever Penny was in the room. Aunt Mary was over the joke but Misti still laughed. She couldn't wait to see how shy Sam dealt with Uncle Bill's dry humor.

Sam arrived early. He had a bouquet of flowers for Aunt Mary and firmly shook Uncle Bill's hand thanking them both for allowing him to come to dinner. When Uncle Bill turned around to head back to the living area, Misti saw Sam let out a huge sigh of relief.

"I've been practicing that all day!" he whispered to Misti.

Dinner went well and Uncle Bill only made one bad wood chipper joke. Aunt Mary liked Sam. She kept offering him more food and looked very interested in what he was saying. Uncle Bill didn't hate him.

"What's your plan for after school, Sam?" Uncle Bill set down his fork to give their guest his full attention.

"I'm going to go to school for IT. I'm hoping to work with computers or technology." Sam left out that he had been hacking his way into people's computers and home security systems for years. Misti thought her Uncle would be impressed by that but Penny probably told Sam to not mentiont his hobby.

Uncle Bill looked unimpressed. "Does that make any money anymore?"

"Starting out is low but I can work my way up pretty quickly. It's only a two-year degree so that will help with the college loans."

Misti knew that Uncle Bill would Google how much someone could make in IT later. She hoped, for Sam's sake, it was a decent amount.

"Do you think it went well?" Penny asked her that night while they got ready for bed. Misti assured her cousin that it had.

The next night, Penny, Misti, and Amber went to Sarah's house. She greeted them at the door, dressed in all black.

"Welcome," Sarah said calmly, opening the door. "Please, come in."

"Why are you talking like that?" Amber asked. Penny and Misti had picked her up on their way to Sarah's house.

"During my research, I found that it is most important to set the correct atmosphere." Sarah closed the door behind them, doing her best to avoid the door making any sort of noise. "Please remove your shoes and follow me."

The three girls looked at each other and tried to not giggle while they took off their shoes.

They followed Sarah down into the basement. Misti was a little disappointed to find Emily sitting downstairs. Misti had not forgiven her for bring Hailey back into Alex's life. Even though she knew it wasn't the little pixie girl's fault. Emily was next to a card table, surrounded by five chairs. Candles were lit everywhere and there was a ouija board on the center of the table along with the diary.

"Pretty sure this is a fire hazard," Amber murmured so only Misti could hear.

"We need to sit in a circle around the table." Sarah motioned to the table. The girls all took a seat. "Please silence all electronic devices. We don't want to scare the spirits."

"What if they scare us?" Penny asked, pulling out her phone and silencing it.

"Just remain calm, no matter what happens." Sarah set her phone up on the shelf behind them. Penny glanced at Misti, looking like she wanted to back out. Misti smiled at her, trying to reassure her. They all placed two fingers on the planchette.

"Lily Banks, we are asking you to come forth and speak to us." Sarah spoke slowly. "Lily, are you here?" For a few minutes, nothing happened. Then the heart-shaped piece under their fingers began to move in a circle.

"Which one of you is doing this?" Amber demanded. Her voice was high, her eyes narrow in suspcsion.

"Shh, remain calm." Sarah did not look at Amber. "Lily, is that you?"

The planchette stopped moving in a circle. Then it slide to the word YES. The air around them seemed to chill. Misti glanced around the table. Sarah was hyper-focused on the wood piece their fingers were on. Emily had a smile on her lips. Penny's eyes were wide with fear. Amber kept glancing at Emily, her lips pursed.

"Is there anyone else here with us?"

A pause before gliding over to NO.

"Lily, were you murdered?"

Back to YES.

"Do you know who murdered you?"

Over to NO.

"Lily, did Brian murder you?" Misti surprised herself when she spoke. There was a tug and the center piece moved to NO. This relieved Misti.

She had only gotten a half-hearted wave from the man at the New Year's party but she felt sorry for him. He was almost trapped by a girl. As if reading her mind, Misti saw the center piece move to LOVED ME.

"Were you having a relationship with Henry Wilks?" Penny asked.

A pause then slide to YES.

"Were you pregnant with Henry's child?" Misti asked.

YES.

"Did he know?"

YES.

"Did he know your plan? To trick Brian into thinking it was his?"

YES.

The responses were coming quickly now.

"Lily, did Henry kill you?"

There was a pause. Then the center thing moved to the letters. DONT KNOW.

"What do you want from us?"

HELP ME.

"How?" Penny squeaked.

A shiver ran down Misti's spine. The air around them seemed to be getting thicker and darker. Looking across the table again, Emily was no longer smiling. Behind her, Misti thought she saw a dark figure, slowly taking shape. She saw slim shoulders, an arm, a hand reaching across towards them.

HELP ME.

"That is so creepy!" Amber jerked her hands away. The air shifted and the figure was gone.

Twenty-Three

A Plan is Formed

"Well, that was...different," Penny said, breaking the trance all the girls had gone into.

"Didn't really help us with anything." Misti leaned back in her chair, scanning the room for the figure. Nothing, not even in the shadows.

"We know that Brian didn't do it now," Sarah said.

"She doesn't know who killed her. He could have done it."

"I think we should trust her," Sarah argued.

"I think someone else was moving the dial." Amber looked directly at Emily. Emily stared back, lifting an eyebrow.

"I was not."

"Then why were you smiling?"

"Because it was cool! She could answer specific questions!"

Amber didn't seem convinced and looked at Misti for support.

"I think we can't rule anything out. This is, after all, something you can buy at Target." Misti flipped the board to show the logo.

"What are we going to do now?" Penny asked. There was a long silence.

"What if we find Shannon and Brian? We know who Brian is. Maybe he knows where Shannon is."

Misti groaned and looked at the ceiling.

"I can't believe I didn't think about this before." She stood and went to the bag Penny had brought along.

"What?" Penny looked alarmed. Misti pulled it open and got out the yearbook. She went back to the table, flipping to the pictures.

She set it down on Shannon's senior picture.

"I know who she is. And it's going to be awkward."

The girls all looked at Shannon.

"She's Alex's stepmother."

The other girls looked, but only Misti recognized the face. She had seen that face countless times over the last few months. Shannon and her pack of walkers came in every Saturday at the same time. They ordered their non-fat drinks and spent an hour cackling in the corner of the shop. They didn't leave tips and often snapped their fingers to get the workers' attention. Abigail hated them.

Shannon had lost a lot of weight since high school. But she still had a short nose and oversized brown hair. And her eyes were the same. Cold and dull. Misti could never put her finger on it, but something was not right with Shannon.

At work the next day, Abigail had gone off to see her boyfriend at the bank and make a deposit. Misti knew she left to avoid Shannon's herd of people.

"Take your time! I can handle this!" Misti told her. She waited, wiping down washed cups and tidying the counter. Right on cue, the walking bunch came in, all wearing coordinating outfits. Today it was pink sweats with dark zipped-up jackets. And ear muffs. There were only four of them. Winter had weeded out the weaklings.

"Just you today? No Abigail?" Shannon scanned the room, looking unimpressed as always.

"Just me. Abigail will be back soon. Had to run some errands for the store."

Shannon rolled her eyes.

"I'll take the usual. Make it a double, though." The others all copied their fearless leader and Misti whipped out their drinks. Just as the older women sat down, Sarah, Penny, Emily, and Amber arrived. Penny looked nervous, but Amber stared hard at the women, eyes narrowing at Shannon.

Misti took her time with her friends' drinks, letting them figure out the best way to attract attention to themselves.

"For the last time, Sarah! There are no such things as ghosts. And besides, the whole murdered-girl-at-prom thing? That's just one of those tales they tell us to keep us out of the parking lots!" Amber announced.

The women's group feel silent, all turning to inspect the teenage girls. Shannon had frozen.

"I'm just telling you what I've seen and heard. Her name was Milly or Allie or something like that. And someone killed her the night of prom. And they never caught who did it. So now she haunts the school, looking for vengeance."

"I don't believe it." Emily took a sip of her tea, glancing at the group of women.

"I heard that she shows up in the mirror and scares people," Misti added as she made Penny's latte.

Shannon was on the edge of her chair, not listening to the compliment the others were giving her about her nails.

"Why do you even care?" Amber asked.

"I heard they found her diary," Penny said. All the girls looked at her.

"Sure, a diary just randomly turns up after twenty years." Amber rolled her eyes. "See you after work, Misti." They all left.

Shannon watched them leave before turning her eyes to Misti.

Misti was cleaning the foaming machine when Shannon's posse stood to leave.

"Go ahead, ladies. I need to use the little girls' room. I'll see you all tomorrow! Pilates!"

The other women all sighed and moved away. Shannon moved to the counter.

"Can I get you something else?"

"What was that obnoxious conversation you and your friends were having earlier?"

Misti pretended to look confused for a moment. "Oh, that. Nothing really. Sarah is just really into the paranormal and she keeps hearing all these rumors about an old ghost haunting the school. Supposedly some girl got killed and no one knows what happened." Misti finished the machine. "I don't believe it, though. Like Amber said, just something to keep us out of the parking lot during dances."

"Oh, Misti, dear, no it is not." Shannon's usual guard fell away and Misti was shocked to see tears well up in the woman's eyes. "There was a girl murdered. Her name was Lily. Lily Banks. And she was my best friend."

Misti's face must have conveyed the correct response, because Shannon grabbed a tissue and dabbed at her eyes, avoiding smudging her makeup.

"It was prom night. Lily and her boyfriend had gone out to the parking lot to…well, you know." Shannon sighed, placing her manicured hands on the counter for support. "They got into a fight and he left her by the car. Then, someone killed her."

"Why would someone do that?" Misti was impressed by her acting.

"That is the big mystery. Lily was a nice girl. A little shy. But never wronged anyone."

"What about her boyfriend? He seems the most likely suspect."

"Several witnesses saw him during the time of the murder. He came back inside." Shannon was twisting the napkin in her hand. Convenient that she wasn't mentioning that she was now married to her dead best friend's boyfriend. "Did they really find her diary?"

"I don't know. I heard that too. But that wouldn't really help, would it?"

"You never know." Shannon shrugged. "Could give more information. She had been secretive the last few months. I felt like something bigger was going on."

"I'm sorry about your friend."

Shannon's wall was going back up. She pulled out a small mirror from her purse, checking that her makeup was all in place.

"It's alright, dear. You just let me know if you hear anything else. Especially about that diary!"

Misti promised she would.Shannon handed Misti a twenty before walking out the door.

Penny picked Misti up a few hours later.

"She kept asking about the diary," Misti said. "And she confirmed everything. Lily was killed. She said they were best friends."

"Why would she want the diary?" Penny scrunched her eyebrows.

"Given what was written in it, she could just want to protect her friend's reputation."

"Or herself. She acted like she didn't know what was going, on but Lily said in the diary that Shannon helped her come up with the plan to frame Brian." Penny paused, stopping at a red light. "Do you think it's odd that she married the guy she supposedly was helping trap in a pregnancy scandal?"

"A little. But it was years later. Brian married someone else and had Alex with her. She died."

"A bad car accident. I remember."

"Alex said cancer."

"Well, yeah. Cancer sounds better than drunk driving. When you're dead, at least."

Misti frowned. Why would Alex lie to her? She was the last person to judge someone based on their mother. And because of Penny, he knew that.

Penny parked the car, grabbing Misti's arm as she was getting out. "I think we need to talk to Alex about all of this."

Misti stared at her cousin. "Why?"

"He's the only way we're going to be able to get into that house. To investigate." Penny sighed. "We're going bowling tonight. Come with us. Me, you, Sam, Alex. We'll talk it out."

Sam arrived to pick up the girls for dinner, coming inside and chatting with Aunt Mary and Uncle Bill while the girls finished getting prepared. Misti was dragging her feet. She did not want to spend time with Alex..

"If you can think of some other way we can get the information we need, then we can do that instead," Penny told her after she had called Sam and told him Misti was coming along that night.

Misti spent the rest of the afternoon trying to figure out another plan. "I don't even know why we're doing this. It's not like we can go to the police and tell them a ghost gave us her diary and asked us to solve her murder," Misti grumbled, changing her shirt again.

"She asked us for help. Don't you think she deserves some justice? Maybe she doesn't need an arrest. She doesn't know who killed her. She might just need that answer."

Misti sighed. Since when was Penny such a good debater?

Sam drove the girls to the restaurant, chatting about some program he was creating, and Penny eagerly nodded along. Misti didn't understand a word he said. Not that she could focus on the conversation.

She had attempted everything to look normal. But everything she put on was either too trashy or too nice. Alex's car was already there when they pulled into the restaurant. He got out and waved to them. Misti saw his face change when she stepped out.

"Did he know I was coming?"

"Nope. Didn't want to ruin the surprise!" Sam winked at her.

"Hey, stranger," Alex said. "How's life?"

Misti smiled at him. If he was upset that she was there, he was hiding it well. "Hope you don't mind; Penny invited me along."

"Not at all. Won't be a third wheel this way."

They moved into the restaurant and waited to be seated. Sam told Alex the same story he told the girls in the car. Alex nodded along. He kept glancing at Misti. It was like he couldn't believe she was standing there.

"I think he's happy to see you," Penny whispered. Misti ignored her.

They sat down at a booth and had chips and salsa placed in front of them. Alex's leg was pressed against Misti's for a moment. The warmth of his leg made her blush and she squeezed herself away from him.

"Do you have to work tomorrow?" Alex asked.

"No; since I work during the week now, I alternate Saturdays and Sundays."

"Cool." A silence fell over the table. Sam didn't seem to notice as he munched on the chips, skipping the salsa. Penny locked eyes with Misti and tried to discreetly nod her head towards Alex.

"What are you two doing?" Alex grinned at them. Penny blushed and hid behind her menu for a second. Misti pulled out the journal and set it on the table. Alex picked it up and thumbed through it.

"What is this?"

"It's the diary of Lily Banks." Alex and Sam looked at her. They did not know that name. "She's the girl who haunts my locker." Sam's eyes darted to the diary and then he looked at Penny.

Alex smirked. "Really? You believe that silly story now too?"

"It's not just a story," Penny defended Misti. "Lily is real."

"Ghosts aren't real." Alex tossed the diary back to the table. Sam picked it up.

"I didn't think so either." Misti was surprised at her calm tone. "But too many things have happened." Penny gave her an encouraging nod and Misti started the story, pausing only to place her order. Alex listened and Misti could tell that he was not buying any word of it. But Sam was on the edge of his seat. He leaned towards Misti, hands crossed in front of him, eyes locked on Misti.

"So you're telling me that a bunch of teenage girls had a little seance and you guys are using that as your proof of ghosts?" Alex rolled his eyes. "Come on, guys."

"It's more than that!" Penny said. "Other things have happened—the dreams, the face Misti saw in the locker. Her things are being arranged. The pie incident at our house."

"I was at your locker all the time. I never saw anything." Their food had arrived and Alex was slicing into a smothered burrito.

"Yes, you did."

Alex stopped eating his burrito.

"Didn't you think it was weird how every time I opened my locker, all of my things were magically ready, no matter what time of day it was?"

"I figured you did that."

"When? You always left the locker with me to go to my classes, met me there at lunch and after school. Those are the only times I went to my locker. Did you see me arrange my things?"

Alex turned back to his burrito.

"Do you remember the time I slammed my hand into the locker? And you asked me what was wrong?" Alex looked at her. He remembered.

196

"I saw her for the first time that day. In the mirror."

"Why didn't you tell me?"

"Would you have reacted like this?" Alex flushed.

There was a long silence.

"I didn't need you or anyone else thinking I was crazy." Misti looked at Penny. "Penny only found out because Lily moved the diary from my things to her desk."

"So, it's not the locker she's attached to. It's the diary," Sam said, picking up the book again. He was so absorbed in the story, he had hardly touched his nachos. He hadn't even looked at his phone once.

"I don't need you to believe in ghosts or the supernatural, Alex." Misti pushed her dinner with her fork. "Maybe just trust us instead. Maybe just believe your friends."

Alex stared at her for a long time, different emotions crossing his eyes.

"Why are you telling us about this now if Sarah, Emily, and Amber are already helping you?"

"Because we're pretty sure that the Brian in the diary is your father. And your stepmother was her best friend."

Alex wanted to read the diary. Misti was reluctant. But, if it led to Alex believing a little more, she agreed.

"What is the purpose of you telling me? Do you think my dad killed her? Because that's not possible." Misti knew that if his father had done it, Alex would not help them.

"No, we don't think that. At least, Lily said she didn't think it was him. Because he loved her."

Alex nodded. Alex offered to pay for everyone's dinner and the group left, heading to the cars. Alex held the diary and was reading the copies of the news story as they walked slowly to the car.

"I thought you'd be here with Hailey?" Penny said suddenly. Alex's didn't raise his eyes from the stories.

"We broke up."

Penny looked ready to burst, coyly smiling at Misti.

"I'm sorry to hear that." Penny did not do well hiding the joy in her voice.

Alex seemed to notice, sighing as he shoved the diary into his pocket. "My dad and Shannon are going to be out of town tomorrow. You guys can come over and search the house. Be a bunch of Nancy Drews. But I really doubt you're going to find anything."

Penny texted Sarah and Amber. Alex turned to Misti.

"Do you want to ride with me? Maybe catch up? I can tell you how horrible my art class is now?"

Misti smiled. "Sure."

It was nice to be back in Alex's car. Misti's heart had started racing the moment he said that he and Hailey had broken up.

"You can ride with me as long as we don't talk about your ghost."

"Fair enough."

He tossed the diary up onto the dash and they followed Sam out of the parking lot, heading for the bowling alley.

"Do you like not having to be at the school in the afternoon?"

"Sort of. I like making money. I'm saving a lot."

"Well, I don't like it."

Misti's stomach flipped backwards. "I'm sorry. I didn't do it to hurt you. I just want to save enough so I'm not scrambling after high school."

"Are your aunt and uncle kicking you out?" The alarm in Alex's voice startled her.

"What? No! I just…" Misti paused. Alex knew a little. She never asked Penny what she had told him and she wasn't sure what Penny knew for sure. "I don't want to be a burden on them any longer than

I have to be. They didn't have to let me come live with them." There was a pause.

"You don't have to explain your story to me. I don't need to know everything that happened. But if you do want to talk about it, I can listen."

Misti felt like telling someone, for the first time since it happened. Sure, she had explained herself to the police and her therapist. But those were both required and she had done it concisely, saying only what was needed.

"It's a conversation for another time. But I would like to tell you." Misti felt a wave of bravery wash over her. "Perhaps we could go out next weekend and talk about it. Just the two of us."

Alex parked in the lot and turned to her, his lopsided grin playing on his lips. "Are you asking me out?"

"I think I am."

They locked eyes. Misti's enchilada did a triple back spin and stuck the landing hard.

"Took you long enough." Alex reached across the center console, pulled Misti to him, and kissed her hard. Misti's body melted into the seat. Cheering outside the car pulled them apart.

Sarah, Amber, and Penny were all jumping up and down. Sam was slow clapping.

Misti blushed and laughed, covering her face with her hands.

Alex drove her home that night, walking her to the door. He kissed her at the door again. It felt like he was kissing her to make up for all the missed kisses over the last few months.

"See you tomorrow, Nancy Drew."

Misti rolled her eyes at him and went inside, smiling. Penny had beat her home but she stood in the foyer, bouncing on the balls of her feet.

"How on earth did that happen?" Penny squealed, hugging her cousin. She and the others had played it cool while they bowled.

"I'm not sure. I asked him to go out with me next weekend and the next thing I know, he's kissing me."

"That's amazing! I'm so happy for you!"

In bed that night, Misti wrote in J.

Dear J,

Alex and I seem to have made up. I didn't realize how much I missed him until he was sitting next to me. I'm ready to tell him everything about Mom and me. I'm so unbelievably happy.

The next day, Penny and Misti went to Alex's house. The others met them there. Just to be sassy, the girls had all agreed to dress like Nancy Drew. Even Sarah arrived in a skirt and sweater.

"Haha, guys," Alex said when he opened the door to them.

"How should we do this?" Amber asked, setting down her purse on the large dining room table. She didn't look much different than she normally did. Sam was trailing after Penny, eyes wide. "Does Shannon have a closet?"

Alex took the girls upstairs and opened the room. It was originally supposed to be a bedroom but it had been made up into the biggest closet that the girls had ever seen.

"Oh, this is what dreams are made of." Amber walked around the room in awe.

"Focus, Amber, we don't have much time!" Sarah said. The groups split up, searching for any suspicious items.

"Do you guys really think you'll find something from twenty years ago? No one hangs onto junk that long," Alex said. He sounded nervous.

"We just need to find her keepsake box," Emily chirped. Even she had dressed up like Nancy Drew, not wearing her usual dark makeup and dark clothes. "Every woman has a keepsake box."

Misti was up on a chair, looking at the top of the shelves. She spotted the box and grabbed it. It had recently been pulled down. The dust line around it was smudged. Opening it up, Misti found a box of paper and pictures.

"Found something!" She stepped down. The group pored over the letters.

Dear P,
  Can you meet me tonight? Usual place?"
  H

Dear P,
  Last night was incredible. I can't believe I am so lucky to have found you. I can't wait until you graduate and we can stop keeping these secrets. Stop by this afternoon.
  H"

Dear P,
  Don't believe anything Lily told you. I promise you it isn't true. She must have found out about us. Come to the usual spot and we will talk this out.
  H

The letters continued on and on. Some older, showing the signs of the initial contact, the continued flirtation. To Misti, it all looked familiar.

"Alex, do you still have the diary?" Misti asked. Alex left, returning a few seconds later with the diary. Misti picked it up and flipped to the start of the flirtation. Picking up on what she was doing, the others started putting the letters in order.

"He was doing this to them at the same time?" Sarah frowned.

"Looks like he started with Shannon first," Amber said, holding up three letters.

"What a sicko!" Emily shook her head.

"Looks like it continued after Lily died, too." Penny held up a dozen letters.

The tone of the letters that came after shifted slightly.

Dear P,

We have to be extra careful now. If anyone else finds out, you might be in danger. We need to stop meeting at the school. Usual spot tonight?

We have to stop meeting for a while now. The police investigation is too close to us. I know we are innocent in this but we must be wise. Let's hold off on meeting. We will talk again after graduation.

There were no more letters after that.

"He dumped her! She graduated and he dumped her!" Penny was appalled.

"She's better off. Sleeping with a teacher. Did she really think that would go well?" Amber was looking through the pictures. Most of them were Shannon and Lily growing up.

"It's statutory rape. A person of power and trust manipulating girls like that." Sarah stood up and looked around the closet but found nothing else of importance.

"This doesn't really give us anything more, though." Penny started refolding the letters and putting them away. Emily had taken a picture of them all.

"It lets us know that the police were investigating him," Sarah offered.

"Or he just told her to end things." Sam spoke for the first time. The girls all looked at him and Alex, who had hung back in the doorway. "I mean, why would the cops be looking at him? Was he at the dance? We know this from the diary, but they didn't know about any of it. And Shannon wasn't going to blab. And your dad didn't know, right?"

Alex shrugged.

"He's never talked about Lily. I can understand why. I'm sure he was the prime suspect."

"Can we talk to him?" Sarah asked.

"No." Alex looked at Misti. "We'll talk to him. Just the two of us. Next weekend."

Twenty-Four

First Date

The next week was pure bliss for Misti. Alex greeted her every morning at her locker with a coffee and a kiss. On the three afternoons she worked, he came by and sat with her during the slow times. Lily had not returned to her locker. Misti hoped she was content with the progress they were making.

"What are the exciting plans for the weekend?" Uncle Bill asked on Friday afternoon. Misti had just gotten home from work and Penny was going to help her pick out the perfect outfit for the evening. She would also be helping prepare questions for Alex's father. Personal and professional, she had said the night before.

"I have a date."

Aunt Mary's eyes shot up from her cookbook and Uncle Bill set down the pile of mail he was sorting.

"Anyone we know?"

"Alex Turner."

Uncle Bill seemed to be remembering the motorcycle.

"I thought you were just friends." Aunt Mary eyes danced the same way her daughter's did when she was excited.

"We are, but I've decided to explore a relationship with him." Misti cracked open a soda and took a slow drink. "He's coming over at 6 to pick me up. He'll come in and say hello first."

"Not on his motorcycle, I hope."

Misti shook her head, smiling before going upstairs to shower and prepare.

Penny had laid out a combination of outfits for her. Misti modeled them all for her and Aunt Mary even joined in for a while. They settled on black leggings with an oversized sweater and brown boots. Misti borrowed Penny's curling iron and added a few bigger waves to her natural ones. She was perfecting her makeup when the doorbell rang.

She hurried down the stairs and found Uncle Bill welcoming Alex inside the house.

"This is from my father; he says hello." Alex handed a bottle of wine to Aunt Mary, who accepted it, eyes wide. It must have been an expensive brand.

Uncle Bill ignored the bottle, eyeing Alex instead. "You will have her home by midnight. There will be no tomfoolery. And if she comes home looking the slightest bit upset or ruffled, I will come find you."

"Yes, sir." Alex glanced at Misti, doing his best to hide his grin.

The car ride to Alex's house was unusually quiet. Up until this moment, there had been no pressure. Now, it was very real.

"Your uncle would probably come hunt me down if I ever upset you," Alex blurted out.

Misti laughed. "Probably."

"Good thing I'm never going to do that to you again."

Misti smiled and placed her hand over his on the center console. "Good."

Alex's father was in the kitchen, cooking. Brian had aged well and Misti could see where Alex got his good looks from. He had the same green eyes as his father, but Misti assumed Alex got his black hair from his mother.

"It's very nice to see you again, Misti. I was told that we already met."

"Briefly, on New Year's Ever." Misti shook his hand before he returned back to cooking. Alex flushed at the mention of that night.

"What have you got cooking, Dad?" Alex pulled out a chair for Misti to sit at the bar. Suddenly, she was very aware that she might be talking to Shannon that night. And her lies from the coffee shop came back to her.

"Spaghetti! Nothing fancy, and who doesn't like spaghetti! It will be a few minutes."

"Where's Shannon?" Misti whispered to Alex.

"Friday night is book club night. Or so she says." Alex shrugged. "Don't worry, she's never home before 10 on these nights. And she typically goes straight to her room."

The sauce was homemade. Misti knew she should get the recipe for Aunt Mary, who was attempting a new spaghetti sauce every other week. But before she knew it their dinners were done and they were moving into the living room.

"So, Misti, Alex tells me you just moved her last fall and live with your aunt and uncle. Where did you live before?"

"Kind of all over. Most recently, Chicago."

"Did you like it there?"

Misti thought about her run-down neighborhood and overcrowded public transportation.

"It was okay."

"Dad, there was a reason we're doing this with you tonight." Alex let his father settle back into a chair. Brian raised his eyebrows, taking a small sip of his wine. Alex looked to Misti and gave her a nod.

"Can you tell us about Lily Banks?"

Brian's face drained of color. A shaking hand set the glass down on the table and he looked at his son.

"How do you know about Lily?"

Misti didn't know where to start or how much she could say. She looked at Alex.

"It's complicated. But Misti has her old locker and one day, she found this inside." Alex stood and went to the bookshelf. He pulled out the diary and handed it to his father. Brian stared at it for a moment before taking it and opening it, handling it like a newborn.

"That's her handwriting." Brian took a long breath in and exhaled quickly. He looked at Misti. "You have locker 31?" Misti nodded. "And this was still in there? It's been over twenty years."

"It just fell among my things one day."

Brian was silent for a long time, flipping through the pages.

"I've not thought about Lily for a long time. But I dreamed about her the other night." Brian set the diary down. "She was beautiful, but looking back, our relationship was so toxic. We were always breaking up and getting back together. I think that's what we thought relationships were supposed to be. Filled with drama." He sighed and picked up the wine again.

"I regretted leaving her like that in the parking lot. We had just had a huge fight and I stormed off. I went back into prom and got the flask my buddy had and downed it. By the time the police arrived, I was out of it. It took them three times tell me Lily was dead before I understood." Tears filled his eyes.

"Why would anyone have wanted her dead?" Alex asked.

"That's the big mystery. Lily was a nice girl but really nothing out of the ordinary. I was just an average guy. She didn't have a ton of friends, besides..." Brian paused, looking upstairs.

"Shannon?" Misti offered.

"Yes. They were best friends."

"Was Lily acting differently in her last few months?"

"You sound like one of the detectives," Brian sighed. "I was interviewed so many times. I can't blame them. Everyone saw us leave together and me come back in alone and act like a jackass." He paused. "She had been different. We had broken up again. For a long time this time. I had actually thought it was real this time. But then, a couple weeks before prom, she called and apologized. She said she wants to go to prom with the only guy she ever loved. That she was willing to make it up to me that night." Brian looked at his son. "You treat her better than I treated Lily." Alex nodded. "Anyway, I knew, afterwards, that I wasn't her first like she was mine. I just knew. And that's why I left her there."

"Lily was pregnant," Misti said, opening to the last few pages and handing the diary back over to Brian. Alex looked nervously at Misti and they watched Brian read.

"Son of a bitch." He dropped the diary on the table and leaned back, wiping his mouth with both hands.

"Dad, I'm really sorry."

Brian focused on his son for a moment.

"Your mother was the only way I could get over Lily. She was so opposite to her. And exactly what I needed. When she died too…" Brian sighed. "I didn't know she was pregnant. And they didn't ever release that to the press. Probably for her family's sake. Do you know who the father was?"

"Not for sure. We know it was a teacher. At least, we assume from the entries. She only ever called him H."

"Henry Wilks?"

"Maybe?"

"Never liked that guy. He was so weirdly creepy with the girls." Brian looked as if a lot of things were suddenly making sense. "Lily was his stage manager. She made a big deal about needing to be available to help him whenever he needed her. It was one of the reasons we broke up again, because she was always working on something for that stupid play."

Henry Wilks had just jumped to the top of the suspect list.

"Dad, we're really sorry to have brought this all up," Alex said.

"No, it's okay." Brian smiled at his son. "It's kind of nice knowing. Things had been so weird with Lily. That night at the dance, she was out of it. I actually caught her outside, throwing up. I figured she had too much of the punch." Brian faded back in time again for a moment, his eyes glazing over as he stared at the diary.

"Come on, let's eat some dessert." They all rose, going to the kitchen.

Alex took the long way back to Misti's house.

"It's crazy to think my father a suspect in any murder. He's such a passive guy."

"He was the last one to be seen with her. He did say he suspected her of cheating on him."

"Her plan wouldn't have worked if she had lived."

"Why not?"

"Because he knew she wasn't a virgin. They would have had to do a test."

"Sounds like a lot of drama."

"Sounds like Lily was a lot of drama."

The ease of conversation was back and Misti rested her hand on Alex's arm, watching him as he drove.

"You look so much like your father."

"Maybe someday I'll get to meet your mother and I can see what you'll look like when you're old."

Misti pulled her hand away looking out the window. She had not thought about her mother often the last few months. The ghost, as weird as it was, had been a nice distraction. She hadn't even thought about seeing her again. They were silent the rest of the way to the house. He left the car running. It was only 11. Still plenty of time to talk.

"You'll probably never get to meet my mom." Misti paused, looking at her hands.

"If you don't want to tell me this, you don't have to."

"No, I want to. I've wanted to tell you for a long time." Misti took a deep breath and found the same bravery she had last weekend. "In September last year, my mother and I moved in with her new boyfriend. His name was Devin. My mom told me he was in sales. That meant he was a drug dealer." Alex's eyes widened slightly. "I was going to school and working two jobs. Devin managed to make rent most weeks, but my job was the only way I could support my mom and I. Anyway. I worked a double that day and was coming home late. It was around midnight. The hall light was out, like it always was. I opened the door to the apartment and there was blood everywhere. Devin was lying in the middle of the floor. My mother was standing over him, holding a knife. She had stabbed him seventeen times." Misti looked at Alex. His eyes were wide. "My mother had a lot of mental problems. They think either bipolar or schizophrenia. She would go into these rages, telling me all sorts of things. One time she tried cutting off all my hair. Another time she hid under the bed for two days because our neighbor's cat was an alien spying on her." Misti felt tears coming down her cheeks and Alex's hands wrapped around one of hers. My mom saw me standing there, and she just started laughing. She told me she had to do it. He had offered her a beer. I screamed and ran to the street. Someone called 911. When the cops got there, my mother tried attacking two police officers with the knife. She cut one of them. They disarmed her and arrested her. And now my mother is in a hospital for the criminally insane. She'll probably never get out."

"I'm so sorry."

"There were always a lot of warning signs. But she was my mom, so all I could do was try to take care of her." Misti turned to him. "If we manage to get through high school and stay together after, I need you to know about all of this. Because whatever was wrong with her could be wrong with me. And if you want to bail now, I will understand."

Alex reached across and brushed away a few tears with his thumb.

"I'm not going anywhere." He kissed her forehead. A weight was lifted from her shoulders. She had finally spoken about it. She had said the words that she was dreading, and now the fear was gone. She didn't need the world to know. But she did want the people closest to her to know.

"You need to stop crying. Your uncle will kill me if you go in with tears."

Misti laughed, wiping them away. "He really would."

Misti had just finished writing in J about the events of the evening when her phone dinged. Glancing at the time, she knew it had to be Alex.

Did you take the diary?

Panic flooded Misti.

No! It was on the table in the living room.

It's gone...

211

Twenty-Five

Discovered

Alex assured Misti that his father had probably taken the diary to bed and he would get it back in the morning. But dread was filling her chest. She struggled to sleep that night and contemplated waking Penny. She decided she might as well let her sleep.

The next morning, Alex texted to let her know that his father had not taken the diary. Alex would sneak into Shannon's closet and room and see if he could find it.

"How was your date?" Aunt Mary greeted her with a stack of fresh blueberry muffins.

"Really great! Had a hard time sleeping." Misti ate a muffin. Aunt Mary smiled at her, sipping her coffee. Misti didn't know if it was because of her opening up last night or what, but before she could stop herself she heard herself asking, "Was my mom always crazy?"

Aunt Mary choked on her coffee.

"Crazy is a harsh term…" Aunt Mary wiped coffee off her lip and up from the counter.

"Aunt Mary. Come on. We both know that, no, it is not politically correct to call someone that. But my mom was crazy. She killed a man because he offered her a beer."

Aunt Mary was staring at Misti open-mouthed. "You've never been this open about this."

"Maybe it's time I was."

"Okay." Aunt Mary put both her hands on the counter. "Your mother started showing signs of mental unrest about the time she turned sixteen. Back then, it was very taboo and my parents did their best to brush it under the rug. I think that's one of the reasons she ran away. Because she was an embarrassment to them." Misti knew what it was like to not have the support of a parent. It wasn't easy.

"Anyway, she turned eighteen, and literally the next day she was gone. I didn't hear from her for almost two years. We were close growing up, but we started drifting apart because of what was happening. I had just turned twenty-two and married Bill when she contacted me. She just wanted to let me know she was okay. She was living in Phoenix at the time. Another two years went by and I had Penny. A letter came this time and it was a picture of you. For a while, I thought she had gotten help. Maybe you were her motivation. But then when you came to visit, I knew that was wrong." Aunt Mary moved around the counter and took her by the shoulders. "I should have done something then. I should have tried to take you then."

"It's okay," Misti said.

"No, it's not!" Angry tears rolled down her face. "I knew you weren't safe. She seemed fine the first few days she was here. But then she slowly started to unravel. I even asked Bill what we could do. He said we could do whatever I wanted. But then you were gone so quickly and I didn't even know where to start. I should have done something!"

"Aunt Mary!" Misti reeled her aunt back in. "There's no way you could have known. And what matters is that you're doing something

213

now. The last few months have been the safest, calmest, and best months of my life. I get to be a teenager. I get to come home to a safe place and eat homemade treats. I am so grateful you are doing something now."

Aunt Mary hugged Misti and they stayed like that for a long time.

Misti told Penny the news about the diary when she woke up.

"What should we do?"

"Alex is going to try and find it. But, if he doesn't, it isn't hard to imagine that Shannon has it and we're never going to see it again."

Alex reported back that the search of his stepmother's room and closet yielded nothing.

"It doesn't mean we stop investigating." Penny patted Misti's arm.

"But how will Lily know? She's attached to the diary?"

"If we figure it out, I'm sure she will know."

At work the next day, Misti was torn. Her personal life was going wonderfully. But the task of finding Lily's murderer had come to a screeching halt. With no way of investigating Henry Wilks, there was not much more the group could do.

"Maybe the diary just went away, like it appeared," Alex said over the phone that night. "Maybe talking to my dad was all she needed." Misti knew he was saying that for her benefit. She agreed with him, hoping that it was true.

It was cold outside and they had fewer customers than they normally did on a Sunday. Happy that she didn't have to make small talk, Misti cleaned every surface, rearranged the pastry display case, washed down all the machines, and organized the tea bags before her lunch break.

"If you want to go home early, you can. I guess even the walking crew isn't coming in today," Abigail said.

Misti frowned. The walking crew had come in, rain or shine, since she started there.

"That's weird."

"It's February. New year's resolutions are on the outs."

Misti texted Penny, seeing if she was free to come get her.

"Take out the trash before you go?" Abigail asked.

Misti zipped up her jacket and called a goodbye before ducking out the back door. She threw the half-full trash bag in the appropriate dumpster, noting that someone else was dumping their trash in there again, before shoving her hands in her pocket and heading down the alley towards the lot. Penny should be arriving at any minute.

The explosion knocked Misti out onto the street. Ears ringing, she pushed herself up and looked around at the coffee shop. The front windows and door had been blown out. Pushing herself up, she ran back into the shop, knees and hands burning.

"Abigail!" She couldn't hear herself screaming. Black smoke was streaming out of the kitchen. Misti covered her mouth with her sleeve and ran to where she had last seen her coworker. She found her lying bloody on the other side of the counter. Misti could not tell if she was alive or not. She leaned down and grabbed her under the armpits and started dragging her out. Glass was everywhere and although Abigail was tiny, Misti struggled to pull her along. Coughing and wheezing in the smoke, she forced herself to keep going. Her lungs, hands, and knees burned. She felt a trickle down her face and heat on her as she pulled her out what should have been the door and onto the street. A couple hands grabbed her and another pair grabbed Abigail. Men from the pawn shop down the street helped carry Abigail to safety. One of them dropped down next to her and Misti watched as they started chest compressions. She turned when someone shook her shoulder. The train store owner was asking her something but the ringing in her ears was more than she could handle.

She was coughing and starting to feel light-headed. She fell back.

Everything went black.

Misti was walking down a white hallway. There were no doors, no windows, no pictures. It was just all white. She felt calm as she wandered, knowing she was safe. She came across a door and opened it. Inside, she found a girl with blonde hair sitting in a chair.

"Hello, Lily."

Lily smiled at her and gestured for Misti to join her. Misti sat in the chair across from the girl. She looked radiant, wearing a blue prom dress, her hair done up.

"I'm sorry about what happened to you." Misti didn't know what else you were supposed to say to a murdered person.

Lily nodded once.

"Where are we?"

"In between."

"In between?" Misti looked around.

"This is the place in between Earth and the afterlife. Most people don't stay here very long. You won't stay here very long. I and others like me are stuck here."

"Why?"

"For a variety of reasons. Unable to accept it, mostly."

"Accept what?"

"Death."

Misti frowned. She was dying? She thought back. Ah, yes. She might be.

"You aren't going to die," Lily said. "But I wanted to thank you while we had the chance. Everyone else over the last twenty years had ignored me. You did not. And because of that I'm almost free."

"What else can I do?"

"Solve my murder. You're so close now." Misti felt a shock in her chest. She gasped.

216

Lily smiled, eyes sad. "I'll see you later!"

The shock jolted Misti again and she was pulled out of the white room, back down the hall. She watched it spiral away.

Misti's eyes flew open. She was in a different white room. She heard faint beeping. Moving her hand to her face, she felt a tube in her nose.

"Misti?" Turning her head, Misti found Aunt Mary sitting beside her. Uncle Bill stood behind her. Penny leaned against her father.

"What happened? Where am I?" Misti's throat hurt and her lungs burned. She started coughing and Aunt Mary rubbed her back, helping her drink water.

"You're at the hospital, dear. There was an accident at the coffee house. They think it was a gas leak."

It all came crashing back.

"Abigail?"

"Alive, but in the ICU. She's alive because of you. They said you ran back inside and dragged her out." Aunt Mary squeezed Misti's hand and stood.

Penny took her place. "The doctor said you have smoke in your lungs. They want to keep you here for a little bit to monitor you."

Misti nodded. Penny unwrapped a cough drop from the table next to the bed and placed it in Misti's mouth. The longer she was awake, the more pain she felt. She looked at her hands, surprised to find tiny cuts all over them. Her knees hurt; she had a headache. The cough drop helped her throat.

"Go back to sleep, dear. We'll be here when you wake up," Aunt Mary said, smoothing her hair. Misti did as she was told.

When she woke, she found Uncle Bill napping in the corner chair. Her throat was a little better but her lungs still hurt. She tried to sit up and started coughing. Uncle Bill woke with a jerk.

"Sorry," Misti whispered between coughs. Uncle Bill got up and got her some water.

"Feeling better?" he asked, sitting on the edge of the bed. Misti shrugged and nodded. Her heachache had subsided and her hands didn't hurt as much.

"Mary and Penny went to get some food."

Misti nodded. She drank all of her water and Uncle Bill filled it up again.

Misti thought back to her first day with her family; how sure she was that Uncle Bill did not like her or want her in his home. How wrong she had been. She covered his hand with hers and he squeezed it, smiling down at her.

"You'll be okay," he told her. Misti smiled back and nodded in agreement.

The next day, Misti was allowed to sit up and started blowing into a device, checking her air capacity. She was low, but the doctors thought she would be able to go home in the next few days. Uncle Bill had taken Penny home the night before. Aunt Mary refused to leave Misti alone and they had stayed up watching the game show network. Uncle Bill returned with coffee for his wife around 8 the next morning. Penny would be coming later.

'You guys don't have to stay." Misti limited her talking. "Go home and get some rest. I'm sure Penny will be along soon." Her guardians protested, but she assured them that she would be fine. After a text to Penny confirmed that she would be there in less than an hour, they kissed her forehead goodbye and said they would be back for dinner.

Misti was glad to have a few minutes alone with her thoughts. She inspected her hands. They would take a few more days to heal, but the tiny cuts all over were not as open as they were yesterday. Misti leaned back and thought about the weird dream she had before waking up in the hospital. Had she really talked to Lily? She must have dozed off because she woke to someone sitting in the chair next to her.

Misti was startled to find it was not her cousin but an older man. She stared at him, feeling around for the call button.

"Hello, Misti. My name is Henry Wilks."

Misti nodded that she understood him.

"As the superintendent of the school, I just wanted to come meet the hero of the city. We are so proud of you, Misti, at Blackwood High." He was different from his picture. His hair was thinner and Rogained. His smile was not charming and there was a darkness in his eyes that made Misti uncomfortable.

"Thank you. I just did what had to be done." Misti found the call button.

"There's another matter I wanted to speak to you about."

Misti kept her face calm, but her heart was racing.

"I know you found Lily Banks' diary."

Misti made no move to confirm or deny it.

"I just hope that you can keep it between you and your boyfriend. No one else needs to know what she wrote. Because, it is, after all, not true."

Rage replaced the fear in her chest. Before she could respond, her door opened. Penny, Amber, Sarah, Alex, and Sam came tromping in. Alex and Sam carried flowers and balloons. The herd of teenagers stopped and stared at Henry.

"Hello!" He stood and shook all of their hands. "I'm Mr. Wilks. Do you all go to Blackwood High?"

They all nodded.

"Aren't we all just so proud of this young lady? So brave, isn't she?"

Henry glanced back at Misti. "I'm thinking we should throw a big assembly in her honor. What do you think?"

Misti shook her head at her friends.

"Misti really isn't into having an audience. So, not a good idea." Amber said, pushing past him and sitting in the chair he had vacated. Henry stared around the room. He had lost his touch with teenagers.

"That's true. Misti would much rather this not be a big deal," Penny smiled. "I don't know if you remember me, Mr. Wilks, but I'm Bill and Mary McGrath's daughter."

Misti wondered what in the world Penny was doing sucking up to this man.

"Yes! Your father was a huge football star in college. I've tried for years to get him to start coaching at the high school. Too busy running his own company!"

"I'm Alex Turner. You probably know my father as well."

Misti rolled her eyes.

Mr. Wilks confirmed that he knew Alex's father.

"Well, I better go, let you all chat with your friend, the hero of the hour!"

He picked up his jacket, having to give it a firm tug to pull it out from underneath Amber. "Again, Misti. We're all very proud of you!"

The teenagers all offered goodbyes. They were quiet for a few moments, waiting for the footsteps to go away from the door. Alex opened it and peeked out, giving a nod that they were good.

"Good cover, Penny!" he said, coming over to Misti. He looked like he wanted to kiss her, but he sat on the edge of the bed where Uncle Bill had been instead and took her hand. Misti wondered how she might look and what deterred him from kissing her.

"Thanks! Did it work, Amber?"

Amber held up a silver key.

Her friends stayed for just over an hour. At first, they discussed the next step in their Scooby Doo-like investigation. But eventually the conversation turned to what had happened with Misti.

"I heard you carried Abigail out over your shoulders!" Sam said, his arms wrapped around Penny from behind. The room was crowded with everyone in it, but no one seemed to mind.

"Haha, yeah, right. I could barely drag her out of there." Misti shook her head.

"Still, pretty cool," Sarah smiled.

"Do you think it has to do with the diary and everything else going on?" Amber asked.

The room went quiet again.

"Freak accident," Alex said. Misti knew he did not like his stepmother, but to think she would do something like this to hide a secret from over twenty years ago was a stretch. But Misti knew that they had just passed their inspection a few weeks before.

"Well, we should probably go. We have a house to scope out." Amber stood. Before she left, she leaned over and gave Misti a side hug. "Glad you're okay."

"Thanks."

Sarah did the same, but Sam just waved at her and Penny smiled. Alex did not get up.

"I'll stay," he told the others. They all nodded, not surprised.

"Good luck!" Misti's voice had grown hoarse with the conversation. And she was tired again. The drugs they had her on were pretty good.

"I'm just going to fall asleep. You don't have to stay," she told Alex as he moved to the chair.

"It's okay. I've always wanted to see what you looked like while you slept." He grinned. "That came out a lot creepier than it was supposed to."

Alex turned the TV on low and Misti fell asleep to the rhythm of commercials, Alex still holding her hand.

Twenty-Six

The Hack

The next day, Misti was deemed well enough to go home but to remain in bed.

Before she left, Aunt Mary and Uncle Bill wheeled her over to ICU, where Abigail was still being observed.

Misti had been told it would be bad, but she was not prepared to see her manager and the woman who had become her friend this way. She was swollen and burned from the initial blast. The nurse wheeled Misti to her bedside and she waited for a few minutes in silence, not sure what to say. Abigail was hooked up to the breathing machine and there were tubes everywhere. Misti felt tears in her eyes but batted them away.

"You must be Misti."

Misti turned to see a shorter man with brown hair and eyes watching her. He wore a business suit and, although she had never met him, she knew this was Ben, Abigail's boyfriend. Misti nodded.

"Thank you. For saving her." He shook Misti's hand. "She was always happier on days she worked with you."

Misti tried to smile but tears started coming again.

"It's okay," Ben told her, handing her a tissue. "You saved her life. And there's no way you could have known it was coming."

Misti nodded, but the idea that this was somehow related to her amateur investigation kept coming back.

Misti insisted on walking into the house and to the couch. She was so happy to be home. She sat on the large sectional, letting Aunt Mary tuck her in and bring her a snack. Uncle Bill gave her control of the remote. Penny came to sit with her.

"I brought your work from school. English only. The others said you could figure it out later. Or they would just excuse you."

Misti decided to look at it tomorrow. She was unprepared for how much the journey home would take out of her. She settled back into the sofa and watched her family move about their daily tasks. And she realized for the first time that this was her family. Not just by blood, but by every definition and connotation that the word had to offer. She smiled while she watched Uncle Bill pester her aunt in the kitchen until she was ready to blow, then swoop in, offering hugs and kisses as a treaty. Penny texted and made gagging noises when he did. This was what home was.

That night, with the help of Uncle Bill, Misti made it upstairs. She insisted on showering alone, knowing that Aunt Mary and Penny waited outside the door, listening for a crash. She took a short shower, happy to wash off hospital. She changed into comfy clothes and climbed into bed. Penny came into her room about five minutes after she finished writing an update in J.

"They're going to sneak in tomorrow. There's a board meeting."

"Will he be there?"

"He's scheduled to give a speech. Sam says it's usually streamed, so they're going to check it before going in to make sure he's really there."

"What if there is an alarm? Or cameras?"

"Sam says he can take care of all of that. He is a hacker, after all." Penny shrugged.

"I don't know if we should do this anymore. What good is it going to do? Even if you find something, which I doubt, there's no way it could be used in a court of law."

"This isn't about the police. It never has been. This is about justice. Lily deserves to know what happened to her and to rest in peace."

Misti remembered the white room and the beautiful girl she had talked to. The one who told her it was going to be okay and that she wasn't dying. She just asked her to finish the search.

"Just tell them to be careful."

The next night, Penny and Misti sat in her room under the guise of watching a movie. Per Sam's instructions, they found the live stream of the board meeting. The agenda was announced, the board members introduced and finally Henry Wilks was smiling towards the camera. Penny texted a confirmation that he was not at home.

Going in, was the response they got from Sam.

"I'm so nervous!" Penny set the phone down. The girls silenced the board meeting and turned on a movie. Ten minutes passed, then twenty. Thirty minutes hit and the board meeting was wrapping up.

Out. No issues. Found some stuff. Video chat in 20.

The next twenty minutes felt more like twenty hours with the girls checking the time while trying to focus on the movie. Misti was anxious. What kind of things could they have found from over twenty years ago?

The phone buzzed once in Penny's hand before she scooped it up. Sam's face was on the screen.

"Hey guys! How are you feeling, Misti?"

"Better, thanks!" Misti half waved.

"What did you guys find?" Penny skipped straight to the point.

"His house was so clean, it was weird." Amber appeared on the screen with Sam. "There was not a speck of dust anywhere!"

"We didn't find anything physical. We only found a computer."

"Everyone has at least one computer now!" Penny was never patient.

"It's more than that. There looked, on the surface, to be nothing there. Just some pictures, a nice background, a couple apps. Typical older guy, not really using his tech. But it all seemed odd. Like, why have this fancy setup and not use it?"

"Get to the point, Sam!" Amber rolled her eyes.

"He's hiding things. His computer is almost full. He has completely digitized his stuff."

Penny smiled.

"Does this mean what I think it means?"

"Yes it does! Yes. It. Does."

Penny didn't know much about her boyfriend's habit of hacking into things. She knew that he only did it as more of a challenge than to do anything malicious. Sam told them all that this could take a while and he would have to find a weakness in Henry Wilks' system. He was certain a tech-savvy guy would have some firewalls and other items in place to keep people like Sam out. He promised to have a full report by Saturday.

Misti spent the rest of the week recovering. On Friday, Aunt Mary took her back for a checkup and she did better on the breathing test. They also stopped by ICU and talked to Ben. Abigail had woken up a few times but they still didn't know much.

Because of her cleaner bill of health, Misti asked permission to go over to Alex's on Saturday for a movie night with friends. Aunt Mary was reluctant but Uncle Bill was on board.

"She's been stuck in the house all week. Let her go have some fun. Penny will take her. And her friends aren't going to let her do anything crazy!"

Alex and Sam were waiting for the girls on the front step. They met them at the car doors. Alex helped Misti out of the car, giving her a kiss hello. She leaned against him, happy to have his warmth against her again. He had been allowed to come over twice this week, under the careful supervision of her family.

"Dad and Shannon are out for the evening." He helped her up the steps.

"Are Sarah and Amber coming?"

"Yeah, they should be here soon."

Alex and Sam set up the media room for them and Misti settled into one of the recliners. Sam's computer was projecting on the screen and Alex was making popcorn.

"Alex and I used to hook up our Playstation and have marathon gaming sessions on this screen. It was awesome!" Sam was looking at Penny, who was watching him with doe eyes. She was crazy about him.

Alex brought Misti a bowl of popcorn and plopped in the chair next to her.

"Sam always won the games. It's one reason I quit. No matter how much I played, I could never compete with him."

"Yeah, you weren't bad though. We killed it in those campaigns. Especially when Tony was still coming over."

Penny's face reddened and she glanced at Misti. Sam was absorbed in the memory and didn't see his girlfriend's reaction.

The doorbell disrupted the conversation. Alex returned with Sarah, Emily, and Amber in tow.

"This is awesome!" Sarah took off her jacket, tossed it to the corner of the room and flung herself into a chair. She leaned back, sighing. "This is so nice." She closed her eyes.

"Sit up, Sarah. We have business to attend to." Amber picked up Sarah's jacket and left the room.

"Geez," Sarah mumbled, pushing herself up. Emily wiggled into the chair with Sarah, giving her a peck on the cheek. Amber returned and went up to Sam.

"Did you get anything?"

"Sure did!" He started clicking on things. Alex turned off the light and sat back next to Misti, wrapping his fingers around hers.

"I knew he would have some things in place to prevent this from being a cake walk. I did eventually get in and I don't need to bore you with the details," he paused, wanting someone to say "bore us with the details." None of them did. "Anyway. We were right. He is hiding something on his computer. But first, his email." Sam pulled up a screen and highlighted the sender's name.

Shannon Turner.

The subject heading was one word: "Trouble."

H,

There are some kids poking around into the old business. They have L's diary. It says everything that happened. What should we do?

P.

The response was simple.

"Get the diary. Handle the situation."

"For a price."

"How much?"

"50."

"Done."

The next email was two days after the diary had been taken.
  "Got it. Send money."

"She does have the diary. She must not have given it to him," Alex said.

"It doesn't appear so." Sam clicked to the next screen.

"I sent the money. Bring the diary."

"No. I want to hold onto it. Insurance."

"Insurance for what? You have more to lose than I do if this comes out."

"I only did what you told me to. Because I thought I loved you and you needed my protection from her. If I go down, you go down with me."

The group was silent.
  "Shannon killed her?" Sarah broke the silence. "Why?"

Sam continued showing the evidence he had found. Henry Wilks had taken videos and pictures of his time with the girls. Lily and Shannon were the first. Shannon actually came first. But then another came. Some pictures looked very recent.

"Turn that off, Sam!" Penny ordered. He did as he was told. "Do we go to the police?"
  "With evidence we hacked and a hazy confession? We would be the

ones who got arrested." Amber pursed her lips.

"This was never for the police. It was for Lily," Sarah chimed in.

"But there's more than just Lily and Shannon. One of those girls graduated last year." Emily looked paler than normal.

"Could we send in the information anonymously?"

Everyone turned to look at Misti.

"I mean, isn't there a hacker collective that does this sort of thing? Hacks people's computers and provides evidence, never giving their name?"

"There are all sorts of groups. They just leak information. Usually against the government or big organizations." Sam started typing away on his keyboard. "But yeah, we could do that!"

Alex squeezed Misti's hand.

"How do we tell Lily?"

"We brought the ouija board," Sarah smiled.

"Great," Alex said. "Things are about to get weird."

While Sarah fetched her board, Alex and Amber gathered candles from around the house. The group moved from the media room to the living room. They lit the candles and set up the board on the coffee table. They all knelt around the table.

"Remember, guys, it's important to have an open mind…" Sarah focused on Alex for a moment, "…and to keep the energy positive." Alex winked at Misti and they all placed their hands on the center tile. After a few moments, it started to move in a circle.

"Lily, are you here with us?"

Misti looked around the table. Sam's eyes were wide, his mouth hanging slightly open. Penny's eyebrows were furrowed in concentration. Amber's jaw was set and Emily had the same smile on her face the last time they did this. Alex's face was expressionless, but Misti appreciated that he was trying for them. The center tile breaking off from the circle forced her to focus.

"Yes!" Sam shouted, hands yanking backwards. Penny shot him a fierce look. "Sorry!" He placed his fingers back on the tile.

"Ask her a lot of questions. We know the answers already. Just to confirm it is her," Amber ordered.

"Lily, did you have a relationship with a teacher?"

YES.

"Lily, did Brian kill you?"

NO.

Alex let out a breath. Did he not believe his father?

"Lily, were you murdered?"

YES.

"Do you know who murdered you?"

The tile stopped moving.

"Did Shannon murder you?"

The tile did not move. The group glanced around at each other.

Twenty-Seven

Closure

"What on earth is going on here?" Shannon's voice broke the tension. "Alex, it's bad enough that you have friends over at all. But now you're playing with one of these? How childish are you?"

Alex's face darkened. The tile began to rotate, much faster than it had before.

"Don't break off," Sarah whispered.

"You children stop this now!" Shannon stepped into the living room. She stumbled, her ankle rolling on her impossibly high heel. She fell onto the ground, her purse flying ahead of her. The diary slid out. Brian appeared then, holding car keys. He looked at his son, confused. Before he could speak, a gust of wind swept across the room, extinguishing all the candles and throwing the diary open. The planchette continued to rotate. The diary began to glow with a green-blue hue. Misti felt her skin crawl and wanted to run.

"Don't let go!" Sarah shouted.

Misti looked at Alex, knowing her eyes were wide in fear.

"It's okay!" he mouthed to her.

Smoke began to pour out of the diary. The smoke began to swirl, then take shape. A hand gripped one side of the book before another appeared, gripping the other side. The group watched as the hands pulled and crawling forward, coming with arms, then a head. The eyes were black, the hair was scraggly. Her mouth hung as if off a hinge. She continued to rise, dressed in her prom dress. Lily Banks stood before them, her dark eyes fading to blue, focusing on Shannon.

Using her bony finger, Lily adjusted her jaw. Misti shuttered when it clicked into place. Her hair turned blonde and she looked almost normal. A girl dressed for prom. But she was not normal. She was floating, glowing.

"You?" Her voice was an echo.

"Lily?"

The car keys fell to the floor. Brian Turner did not look frightened. Shannon had grown pale, her eyes shining, her mouth hanging open in a half scream.

"How could you?" Lily asked. She did not seem to hear Brian. Shannon snarled, losing whatever fear she had felt before and pushed herself up.

"Because you deserved it. Because you always got everything I wanted. You and Brian were never happy. I would have made him happy. I have made him happy now! But no, you had to date him. But only after I told you that I liked him. And then, I find someone new. And then you have to have him too. And on top of it all, you get to have his child? And ruin it?" Shannon pushed herself to stand. "I killed you to save both of them!" Shannon swung around to the group, focusing on Misti.

"I thought you were the one behind this all. I rigged the shop to blow. It's amazing what you can learn from the internet. Accidentally gas leak! No one was supposed to be hurt but you! Abigail wasn't supposed to be there! She's always out at that time!"

Lily turned to look at the teens for a moment. Her blue eyes met Misti's. She let jaw drop and her eyes went black. The beautiful girl who had appeared began to morph into a decomposing body. Her hair became strings and her skin turned a sickening blue. She rose, letting out a piercing cry. A black mist descended upon Shannon. Misti turned away, squeezing her eyes shut, wishing she could close her ears to the screams.

When they stopped, Misti peeked and saw Lily had returned to her prom night self, looking at Brian. Shannon was gone.

"I'm so sorry for leaving you that night, Lily," he said, tears in his eyes. "If I hadn't left. If we had just stayed in the car."

"It isn't your fault, Brian. I forgive you." Lily's eyes glistened. "I'm sorry for everything I ever did to you."

Lily began to fade. She turned back to the group.

"Thank you." Tears were streaming down her face and a she looked up, smiling at the ceiling. She lifted her hands and slowly faded away.

Two months later, Misti was almost back to normal, eating cereal in the kitchen, listening to the news.

"Breaking news! Henry Wilks, Superintendent of Blackwood School District has been arrested and charged with statutory rape, sexual misconduct by a person in power and solicitation of murder." Aunt Mary gasped. "He is also suspected in the suspicious death of Shannon Turner, who was found in the high school parking lot two months ago. Shannon Turner had disappeared from her home and was reported missing by her husband, business owner Brian Turner. An apparent suicide note had been found on her pillow, leading police to investigate Henry Wilks. Mr. Wilks' attorney could not be reached for comment. Wilks was arrested outside his home yesterday evening. He was booked into the county jail, a $25,000 bond was issued by the judge."

The commentators went on to say more but Misti turned back to her cereal, feeling satisfied. Lily had not been heard from since that night. She was finally at peace. Any arrest was only protecting future victims. Besides, it was prom that night and she was going to get her nails done.

"How awful!" Aunt Mary turned off the TV. "To think I served that man at many a BBQ!" She disappeared upstairs, probably to discuss the news with Uncle Bill.

The phone began ringing while Misti was putting her dishes in the dishwasher. She grabbed it.

"Hello?" She wiped her hands on her jeans.

"Misti?"

She had not heard that voice in months but Misti recognized it.

"Hey Ms. Webb," Misti smiled at Aunt Mary who came jogging back down the stairs. "What's up?"

"Misti, I'm just calling to tell you that your mother has taken a plea deal and is being placed in a correctional facility in Kansas. She asked that you be informed." There was a pause. Aunt Mary stood by, arms crossed, eyes wide.

"Okay." Misti processed the information. Kansas was not too far away. Ms. Webb told her which one and Misti wrote it down. Misti thanked her.

"Oh and Ms. Webb," Misti looked at Aunt Mary. "Thanks for the advice. About making this a new start." Misti thought she heard the robot woman smile. Misti stared at the address for a long time before speaking. Aunt Mary pretended to clean up in the living room, glancing over at her several times.

"They put my mom in a correctional facility in Kansas."

"Oh?"

Aunt Mary must have already known. Misti herself had not been following her mother's case but she had a sneaking suspicion that her Aunt and Uncle were keeping close tabs on it. That response had confirmed her hunch.

"What would you like to do?" Aunt Mary asked.

"I don't know. I need to think about it." Misti excused herself up to her room. She sat on the bed, mulling over the news. Her therapist had suggested again to call her or even go see her. But Misti was not ready for that yet. She also wondered if her mother was finally getting the help she needed. If she was, seeing her might hurt that process right now. And if she wasn't, any phone call or visit would be a waste of time.

Misti pulled out her journal.

Dear Mom,

I want you to know that I am okay. Aunt Mary has done a really good job of taking care of me. Uncle Bill has taught me how to drive and in the fall, I plan on going to college. I've learned to cook and even have a boyfriend. His name is Alex and he is so sweet and kind. We are going to prom tonight. Aunt Mary, Penny and I went dress shopping a few weekends ago. I also have made some really good friends here. Amber is going to a school in Fort Collins and Sarah is going to a local college so I will at least see her. Alex is going to the same one as Sarah. Penny is still undecided and I think Uncle Bill is ready to make the decision for her.

Penny has become a sister to me. We tell each other everything and even when she is driving me crazy, I still love her. I hope she stays at the local school too. I will miss her if she doesn't.

I hope you are doing better. I hope you write me.

Love, Misti

Misti closed her journal. She wasn't ready to send it today. Maybe tomorrow, maybe the next. Penny knocked on the door.

"Misti! Come on! We need to go!" She heard Penny running down the hall. Misti didn't know what to do about the letter. But she did know she had a dance to get ready for.

* * *

"Smile, girls!" Aunt Mary held up her phone, squinting as she attempted to take a picture. Misti and Penny were standing on the front steps of the house. Penny was in a purple knee-length dress with tulle and sparkles. Misti had gone for an elegant blue floor-length halter top. They had practiced updos on each other for weeks.

"Now one with your dates!" Aunt Mary waved the boys back into the shot. Sam was wearing a gray suit and purple vest that matched Penny's dress. They were unable to get him out of his Converse, though he had changed the laces to purple.

Alex looked gorgeous in his black pants, vest, and blue tie. The boys stepped behind the girls. Alex rested his hand on Misti's hip. Brian Turner stood behind Mary, sipping the beer Uncle Bill had offered him when he arrived.

The limo arrived with a short honk. Sarah and Amber popped out of the top, waving at them.

"Have fun!" Aunt Mary told the girls, giving them each a quick hug and kiss on the cheek.

"Keep them safe, boys!" Brian said.

"Will do, Dad." Alex shook his father's hand before climbing in after the girls.

The group laughed all the way to the dinner, through dinner and the dance.

Near the end of the night, Misti and Alex were slow dancing, her arm up against his chest and hand resting on his shoulder. Lost in deep thought, it took her a moment to realize Alex was talking to her.

"Are you okay?"
"Yes, just thinking."
"About what?"
Misti smiled at him.

Afterword

Thank you for reading this novel. I hope you enjoyed reading it as much as I enjoyed writing it. I have always been fascinated with any ghost story I have heard and hope to continue to share my love of the paranormal with you in the future.

I would appreciate a review, letting me and other readers know what you thought of this novel.

If you liked what you read, please subscribe to my newsletter, follow me on Facebook or Instagram to stay up to date on upcoming novels. I also maintain a blog if you would like a peek into my writing process, inspiration and life as an aspiring author.

About the Author

Deidre Bjorson lives in Colorado with her husband and their 3 fur babies. When she is not writing, she spends her time camping, fishing, paddle boarding, hiking or simply enjoying the sunshine. *The Haunting of Locker 31* is her debut novel. Visit her Facebook page, or subscribe to her newsletter to stay informed about her next novels.

You can connect with me on:

🌐 https://bjorsonbums.com

📘 https://www.fb.me/deidrebjorson

Subscribe to my newsletter:

✉ https://mailchi.mp/f75196865392/deidre-bjorson

Made in the USA
Las Vegas, NV
06 October 2023

78684968R00152